WE SHOULDN'T HAVE COME HERE

Five friends. A tropical storm. And a nightmare they never saw coming.

By Sara Kate

Printed in the United States of America.

For more information, or to book an event, contact: **www.sarakateauthor.com**

ISBN - Paperback: 979-8-9921684-2-6

ISBN – Ebook: 979-8-9921684-1-9

First Edition: APRIL 2025

WE SHOULDN'T HAVE COME HERE

PROLOGUE

NOW

MADISON

Seeing a dead body is traumatizing. It's even more traumatizing when you knew the victim, regardless of whether you were close to the person or not. Then when you think the weight of their death falls on your shoulders, that kind of guilt becomes almost impossible to bear.

A drunk idea always sounds like a great idea at the time. But until you are met with the consequences of your own drunkenly actions that sober you would never do, you realize you didn't have such a great idea at all.

Sober me would have let my brother and our friends explore an abandoned prison without me. But drunk me decided to live recklessly the night we all went out to help Danny get through his father's death.

But although the night quickly became a blur, one thing I can clearly remember is the eerie feeling that crept upon me while we were exploring the abandoned prison. The feeling was very subtle, yet also very present—like there were six of us instead of only five.

At the time, I chalked it up to the spirits of the dead inmates who died in the prison during a fire years ago. I even told myself I was feeling the spirit of Danny's father who recently passed away. After all, his dad's death was the reason we were there that night. We only wanted to help Danny grieve and get through another parental loss.

But I was wrong about potential spirits watching over us that night. Television shows and movies teach us to be scared of the dead, except the dead can't harm us. It's the living who we should always be most fearful of.

But sadly, my friends and I did not think about that until it was far too late.

3 DAYS EARLIER

SATURDAY

1

DANNY

SATURDAY - 12:45 p.m.

*He's gone and now so is his damn ring—
The last thing he ever gave me. The last piece of
him that I can hold on to. What a way to keep my
father proud from beyond the grave.*

Noticing I lost my father's college class
ring after getting shitfaced drunk the night
before is not a fun realization during a
hangover the next morning. Especially since
he gave me the damn thing only two weeks
ago, right before he died in the ICU.

"You alright, man?" Oliver leans against
the doorframe, sipping on a beer as I pace the
bathroom in our two-bedroom apartment.

I'm surprised to see him awake at only
a quarter to one o'clock in the afternoon.

Normally, the unemployed fuck sleeps in until at least two or three o'clock instead. Especially after a night like we had at the bar with our friends last night.

"You look like you need a beer." Oliver nudges me while I look for the shiny piece of missing gold on the floor.

His suggestion automatically irritates me. No more beer. No more alcohol for me for a while. Or at least, not until I find my father's ring. I can't be this absent minded. I *need* to find it. I know I wore it on my finger last night because I haven't taken it off since my dad gave it to me. I already searched my entire bedroom for the ring, including stripping the bed sheets and blanket off the bed. I even checked the pocket of my jeans from last night. Maybe I dropped it somewhere behind the toilet last night after we got home and I didn't realize it.

"When was the last time we cleaned back here?" I turn my nose in disgust when I lean down to search behind the toilet for the ring on the floor.

Oliver shrugs. "Don't think we've ever cleaned in here at all. My ass just touches the toilet seat and that's all I care about." He chugs the rest of his beer and crushes the can. "We should hire a cleaning lady."

I ignore his idea. I should have ignored him last night when he convinced all of us to break into an abandoned prison too. I also shouldn't have listened to Oliver two years ago when he came up with the brilliant idea to become roommates. I never had a problem living with him until three months ago when he stopped paying rent after he got fired from his job.

The kitchen. I slightly remember eating a bag of chips when we got home.

"Have you seen my dad's ring anywhere?" I ask Oliver as he follows me to the kitchen and grabs a second beer out of the fridge which is adjacent to our living room.

"Nah, man. When's the last time you remember seeing it?" Beer in hand, Oliver walks into the living room and lifts up the couch cushions in an effortless attempt to help me look.

God forbid, he put the drink down for a minute.

"I wore it last night when we went to the bar."

The events of the night merely replay in my head like a time jump. Besides listening to Oliver's idiotic idea to explore the partially burned down prison that has been abandoned for seven years, I barely remember anything. We all took an Uber to the bar, had a few drinks (okay, a lot of drinks) and then walked to the prison.

It wouldn't surprise me if my dumbass self lost it in my drunken state of mind...

Then again, even while intoxicated, I would think I would have noticed the absence of the ring on my finger. I've been fiddling with it like a nervous tick ever since my dad gave it to me. I think it would have been obvious to me if I had dropped the ring at one point throughout the night. I need to try to retrace my steps.

After shooting back way too many shots and downing a lot of beers, we found ourselves leaving the bar to walk two miles to the prison. We didn't call an Uber to take us there because in our drunken state of minds, we decided a two mile walk in the Everglades on a dirt road would be a better idea.

The walk to and from the prison, and actually spending time in the building is erased from my memory, but I know we walked back to the bar to get picked up by an Uber to take us home afterward.

I hope I didn't drop the ring while we were walking...

There's no chance I'll find it if that's the case. The Everglades are unforgiving when it comes to finding something as small as a ring. The rain from last night won't help me find it either. Not that I woke up or remember hearing the rain come down at all. I can only tell it stormed sometime after we got home because of the wet pavement outside of my apartment and the slightly flooded parking lot.

If the ring is on the side of the road, then the only thing my father has ever given me is most definitely gone— either washed away into the lake, hidden in between the mangroves, or buried deeply into the mud already.

A hurricane is supposed to hit the east coast of Florida, opposite of us (we're on the Gulf coast) tomorrow afternoon, so if the ring is anywhere outside, I've probably lost it forever. But until I search this entire apartment, I can't lose hope just yet.

While looking through the kitchen cabinets, my phone buzzes. Jane, the new woman I started dating a few weeks ago—exactly five days before my father suddenly died, just texted me.

Jane: *Good morning!*

Her second text follows with a sexy selfie while holding her cup of coffee on the couch. I'm glad I checked my phone because for the first time since I woke up this morning with a raging headache, I find myself smiling. Not only is Jane beautiful, she's also dealt with the rollercoaster of emotions that I've been trying (and failing) to hide following my dad's sudden passing.

I compliment how beautiful she looks with a *good morning* text back before my eyesight drifts up to the message I sent her last night. To my horror, in my drunken state of mind, I sent her a not so flattering group photo of my friends and I in one of the holding cells. Acting as if we were inmates ourselves. *Thankfully, she never acknowledged the picture.*

I look like an idiot, at thirty years old, trespassing into a place I have no business being in with the rest of my thirty-year-old friends. Good thing I just answered her text message now. At least she knows that I am awake and coherent.

I assume she never answered my text last night because there wasn't much to say. She's probably giving me a pass for acting like a child due to the recent tragic event in my life. I'll thank her for being so understanding later.

My phone buzzes again.

Jane: *How's the hangover going?*

Clearly, she knew how intoxicated we all were. Before responding, I zoom into the photo to see if my dad's ring is on my finger and there it is.

Fuck me. I slump down on the couch. My back lands uncomfortably against the hard back of where the cushions should be, but are still laying on the floor, thanks to Oliver. "I either lost the ring while we were walking or it's at the prison."

"No way, dude." Oliver sits next to me. "You sure, you don't want a beer?"

"Nah, man. Look. I had the ring on in this picture that I sent Jane."

He glances at my phone and laughs. "Damn, we were trashed. What a night."

His comment aggravates me. Although, he's right. The last time I got that wasted had to be at least a year ago or more. My friends only decided to get me drunk to distract me from my father's death for a night. Their plan worked, until it didn't this morning.

I need to look through more photos and videos. If the ring is off my finger at any time throughout the night, then I definitely lost it in the prison. If that's the case, then I rather have lost it there, instead of losing it on the side of the road. There is a better chance I'll get it back then.

I swipe away from mine and Jane's conversation to my gallery to see more evidence from the night. Four videos and three photos help me start to remember. One of the photos being the one I sent to Jane.

Oliver huffs a laugh when I play a video of Madison writing her name on a wall under a sign that says *Medical Center* with a sharpie. Oliver pauses the video, suddenly in deep thought. "Where'd she find that sharpie?"

"I don't fucking know, man."

Leave it to Oliver to ask an unimportant and irrelevant question at a time like this.

Besides the group photo, I am not in the rest of these because I took the videos and photos from my own phone. I need to rely on Oliver's photos and videos which had to be a lot more than what I captured. He is the only one out of our group that posts everything on social media—especially things people don't necessarily care to see. *His food. Random objects on the road. Empty beer cans.* The list goes on.

"I got a video of Lucas pushing you around in a wheelchair, like you were a crippled inmate," he says.

I grab his phone and pause the video to zoom in on my hands, which are gripping the sides of the wheels of the chair. *There it is! My dad's gold class band shines around my finger.*

In the next video, Eric, Madison, and Lucas toss a basketball at each other in a hallway where the walls are charred from the fire. Madison screams as she dodges the ball when it misses her head by only a few inches.

Oliver chugs the rest of his beer while I continue to look through his phone. I stop on a photo of Madison and Oliver together, alone. Well, I don't recall the two of them going off by themselves but the evidence is here. Eric, Lucas, and myself are nowhere near them in this picture. I wonder what Eric thinks about that. That is, if he even remembers.

In the last video from the night, I watch myself stumble out of a cell in an attempt to scare Oliver which I succeed at doing because he drops his phone right after my appearance. Before the video ends, I catch a glimpse of my shoes on the screen when he picks the phone back up again and stops recording. I replay the video, and hit pause right before he drops the phone. Although the screen is blurry, I see the absence of the shiny gold band from my right hand as I hold onto the frame of the doorway.

Well, fuck me. I really did lose the ring in the prison.

If my dad were alive, he'd kill me if he knew I lost it already, especially in an abandoned prison. Of all places. Then again, I wouldn't even have the damn thing if he were still living. I shouldn't have been wearing it to begin with. I should have stored the ring somewhere safe instead. Dad's probably looking down at me, shaking his head. Although I've never failed him while he was alive, I definitely failed him now while he's dead. And that feels a lot worse for some reason.

"Guess I know where I'm going after work tonight," I mumble. The thought of trespassing in the prison again— this time, consciously sober at my age makes me cringe. Drinking again would defeat the purpose for my mission this time around. Although, liquid courage *would* make me feel less cringey.

"Really?" Oliver asks as if he doesn't understand the importance of losing the ring. Then again, of course he doesn't understand this situation because he still has two perfectly healthy, nondivorced and alive parents. The man is behind on rent, drinks half the day, and rarely takes anything seriously. Of course, he won't understand what I am going through right now.

At thirty-one years old, I can't see how Oliver lives his life with no future plan. And no present plan either. Oliver's been my best friend for almost two decades now and more times than often, he acts like the brother I never had. That's why I can't get rid of him. Not that I would ever want to, no matter how much he aggravates me.

Stereotypically, between the two of us, I should have become the one that doesn't have my life together at this age. Even though my parents never divorced, our small family ended shortly after I turned five years old. My mom died from breast cancer which sent my father into an alcoholic spiral for years until his death just two weeks ago.

Dying from an unexpected car wreck by a drunk driver while he was sober was not how anyone imagined my father's life would end. Talk about irony. Or maybe, call it karma? I don't want to say my dad deserved to die, but he wasn't a saint when it came to drinking and driving either.

I would go back to the prison to look for the ring right now, but work is more important since I am the only one keeping a roof over our heads. My job at Captain Dan's airboat tours has its benefits. One of them being that my shift starts at two o'clock in the afternoon and ends at ten o'clock. I don't have to wake up early and I get to enjoy the outdoors all day.

If my dad's ring is still at the prison which it should be, then it's not going anywhere until I get there tonight.

"Well, I ain't got nothing better to do. Pick me up on the way," Oliver volunteers.

I know he only wants to go back, simply so he can act like the teenager he never learned to grow up from. Doesn't matter to me. I need the help tonight anyway. He better not be drunk by the time I pick him up though or else I'll leave his ass home.

"Sure, but be ready by ten. I don't plan to stay there long. I just want to get my ring back and then meet Eric at the gym."

"Gym douchebags."

Oliver has never lifted a weight or stepped foot on a treadmill ever in his life, which is completely opposite from mine and Eric's lifestyle. How we're friends with him is beyond me sometimes.

Had I known the decision to go back to the prison would lead us to the second worst night of my life—my father's death being the first (My mother's death doesn't make the list of worse days; I was too young for it to be more than a story I've been told rather than a memory I own.)— I would have let the ring go and accepted that I am a terrible son for losing it.

But we did go back.

And I'm not sure if I should regret our decision or be relieved about the outcome.

2

O L I V E R

SATURDAY - 1:30 p.m.

The key to getting over a hangover is to stay drunk and you won't feel the effects of the alcohol the next morning. Nobody ever listens to me when I tell them to keep drinking. I swear, it works. I've been doing it for years. Danny should have had a beer before he left for work just now. A beer would have calmed him down.

The man has really received the shit end of the stick in life. Hearing his dad suddenly died from a car wreck is unbelievable. Everyone always thought he would die from the alcohol. Hearing that another drunk driver took the man out instead of his own booze was a shock to not only Danny, but to all of us too. Seeing his dad die in the ICU had to been rough on my man. It only took a few hours after the accident for him to kick the bucket. Something about a delayed hemorrhage or ruptured spleen.

Shit, it was rough on me when I went to visit the guy. I could only take a few minutes of seeing his dad lay helplessly while Danny sat next to him. I respect Danny for having to go through that after already living his whole life without his mom. Honestly, I probably would have offed myself by now if I were him.

I can't even imagine what the hell could be going through his mind lately but losing the ring seemed like it really fucked him up this morning. I don't remember seeing him drop it last night or take it off, but I can't really remember much of last night anyways, so it'll be fun to head back tonight. Besides, I can't let Danny go back alone. After all, it was my suggestion to go there in the first place so I feel the responsibility to accompany my buddy tonight. I know you can't make a man forget about a dead guy, especially his own father, but I think we did a good job at distracting him from everything by getting him drunk.

We should gather the gang up again, but I know it'll be pointless to ask everyone. They're all going to say no because they'll use some lame excuse like having to work the next day.

While replying to the comments on our picture in the prison that I posted on my profile last night, my phone rings.

AMY CALLING.

This bitch again. I am not in the mood for her bullshit right now. I ain't ever in the mood for her anymore. I mean, what the hell really goes through her mind when she calls me over and over and over again? Literally back-to-back calls within only a few seconds apart from each call. I didn't answer the fifteen missed calls from last night, so then what makes her think I want to answer the phone now?

I swipe up on the ignore button and continue scrolling through my feed, but my phone rings again.

AMY CALLING.

While grabbing a beer from the fridge, I reluctantly hit accept on the call. If I keep ignoring her, she'll just keep blowing my phone up and I'm not in the mood to deal with that today.

"What's up?" I groan.

"Are you coming to my sister's wedding with me this weekend or not?" She demands.

"Well, hello to you too."

No hello, how are you? How's your day going? Nothing. It's always a demand out of her.

"Seriously, are you coming with me or not? You didn't answer me at all last night and my sister needs to know if I'm bringing someone with me. The wedding's in a few days."

The anxiety in her voice is loud. I hold back my laughter. Anxiety isn't funny but whenever Amy is anxious, it can be kind of comical to me. She's naturally spazzy. Always uptight and complaining about something.

"Nah, I'm busy. Take someone else."

"Fine. Thanks for being the jackass you normally are."

"You're welcome." I sip my beer and hear the click of the phone call ending.

Dressing up for formal occasions is not my style. Hell, I ain't ever been to any fancy get-togethers, let alone a wedding and I sure as hell don't want the first wedding I attend, be the judgmental family of my girlfriend. Well, ex-girlfriend.

Who knows what we are anymore? I do know that we're just that type of couple who need space from each other... a lot of space. A lot of space... all the time. We can't go more than a day without an argument. I really have no desire to be with her anymore, but I also don't *not* want to be with her either. I know it's selfish of me— to string her along when I'm not really in love with her, but the sex is too good to give up.

It ain't that good enough for me to get dressed up and sit through a long wedding with a bunch of judgmental people though. She can ask someone else. Amy denies being with other men, but the truth is in her social media posts. Also, the influence of her female friends does not help our relationship or situation (whatever you want to call it) either. When she has a bunch of hypercritical women who are in their own toxic relationships, spewing hate against me in her ear all the time, it's kind of hard for her to actually learn how to love me.

The only times we're good together is after a couple drinks. Last night was an exception to that fact though. I was too shitfaced to meet up with her after I got home from the prison which is why I ignored her all night.

Judging by the fifteen missed calls, seeing her in person after having such a great night with my friends would not have been a smart idea on my end. If I talked to her last night, I would have ended up at her place and woken up to her in my face begging me to go to the wedding, instead of denying her over the phone. Much easier this way.

See, even when I'm drunk, I can still make good choices. I have no idea why my friends always say otherwise. Last night, I made a good choice when I took us to the abandoned prison. Surprisingly, my friends thought so too.

Back when we were teenagers, I brought us to a couple rundown buildings like the prison. Danny, Lucas and Eric never said no. Maddie always did though. When it came to trespassing, she worried about the possibility of getting arrested and if that were the case, she always said she'd bail us out. Thankfully, that never happened. Any other time when we were not breaking the law though, she was always with us.

Last night was the first time we went back to an abandoned building in our adult years. The alcohol played a huge factor in my friend's decision to say yes to me, but so be it.

I need to get them all that drunk again soon so they can say yes to more of my crazy adventures. Especially Maddie. She's funny when she is shitfaced. I've seen her drunk many times before but not as bad as she was last night. I am actually surprised that she went to the prison with us but then again, she was so out of it, I know she wasn't thinking straight. And I'm glad she wasn't. She's more fun when there are a few drinks in her. Speaking of Maddie, she should be getting off work in an hour. Perfect time to go visit her.

There's no food in this fridge per usual and I'm starving. If I ride my bike over there now, I'll catch her just in time to piss her off before her shift ends. She hates working morning and lunch shift because of how busy the diner gets and it's fun to aggravate her. It'll be even more fun because I know she's got a hangover.

Flirting with her is also entertaining. I know that's not the best idea of mine, unless I take it seriously with her because of Mr. overly protective big brother Eric, but so be it. Eric's one of my best friends. He can trust me. Besides, I should be trying to get over Amy anyways.

I walk out of my apartment and lock the door from the inside before shutting it. Since my car got repossessed last month, it's become a habit of mine to forget my keys so I started keeping my apartment key under the doormat. I don't need keys to start a bicycle and if I carry just one key by itself, I'll lose it. If Danny knew about that, he would flip out on me. He thinks it's unsafe to leave the apartment key under the mat— as if a burglar will automatically know to lift up the rug, find the key, and let themselves in. Especially in this small town. Burglars aren't just roaming around here.

While biking the mile over to the diner, my phone buzzes.
NEW TEXT MESSAGE

AMY: *Sorry I hung up on you but you can be a real dick sometimes.*

Amy has an employee discount at Lester's Restaurant even on her days off, so I know she'll pay for our dinner.

OLIVER: No worries. I can see you tonight for dinner before I go help Danny out after. He lost his ring last night at the prison. I'm gonna help him look for it after he gets out of work. Meet at Lester's at 7 pm?

AMY: Fine. Don't be late.

I wish I never talked my friends into going to the abandoned prison the night we all got drunk. If I hadn't brought us there in the first place, Danny wouldn't have had to go back for his ring. No one would have died because of my choices. And no one would have gone through more trauma than what Danny had already endured.
This was all my fault.

3

M A D I S O N

SATURDAY - 2:00 P.M.

Working an eight-hour long shift is not the best cure for a hangover. That is, if this is even a hangover. I did sleep off the alcohol for a few hours before waking up at six o'clock this morning to start my shift, but I still feel a bit tipsy.

Although last night was eventful and admittedly a good time, I am now facing the consequences for not having any girl friends. I sometimes wonder what my life would be like if I hung out with women as opposed to just my brother and male friends. Would a woman suggest trespassing in an abandoned prison after drinking the night away at a bar as a form of hanging out?

I'd like to think not.

Maybe we'd go to the spa and get our nails done, get our hair done, or worse than that— dance at a club or a bar with random guys we've never met and shouldn't trust.

Hmm, then again, maybe hanging out with the guys *is* overall a safer bet.

The thought of having girl friends always quickly leaves as fast as it appears in my mind anyway. The last and two times I had a girl friend, happened over ten years ago. Neither times, did the friendships pan out to be that type of "sister friendship" you see in the movies and on TV. You know, the women that remain friends into adulthood who can supposedly rely on each other because they've been friends since kindergarten, then end up being bridesmaids at each other's weddings thirty years later.

If I ever get married, I imagine my future sister-in-law will take the place of my bridesmaid. Unless my future husband is an only child or even better, his sister won't like me for no good reason either. Then Eric will have to fit himself into a dress and stand behind me with the bouquet.

The lack of women friendships in my life is the reason why I have always hung out with my brother since we were teenagers. Although I am two years younger than him, Eric has never objected to me tagging along with his friends as we grew up. Simply because, he knows I've always struggled with making my own friends.

Even though I enjoy hanging out with the guys, a night like last night should not happen again. It wasn't the first time I got drunk with them and it won't be the last, but it was definitely the first time in a while that I got *that* drunk. Drunk enough to say yes to trespassing in an abandoned building in the middle of the night at twenty-nine years old. If I were sober, I wouldn't have gone with them.

As teenagers, Eric and our friends explored abandoned places, always courtesy of Oliver's suggestions. Never did I go along with their dangerous excursions back then, yet somehow as an adult, I made a childish decision. I blame the alcohol.

"Madison. You got a new customer on table twelve. You better get to him or else Alana will blame me if he complains." Megan, the server trainer which is just a fancy word for *restaurant floor manager* who still serves food to the tables, forcefully steps in front of me to grab a plate of food off the kitchen line. She is terrified of our manager, Alana. I on the other hand, don't give a shit about Alana. Worrying about others is not worth my mental health. I'm not scared of anybody, especially a woman my age with a bad attitude.

And speaking of not letting anyone affect my mental health, Oliver sits at table twelve with a devious smile. *Why the hell is he here again? I'm too tired and hungover for his nonsense today.*

Oliver showed up last week before my shift ended, like right now. It's like he timed his arrival perfectly— thirty minutes before my shift ends. I know he's here for his own entertainment. He finds joy in irritating me while I work. That, and he probably wants a free meal. I told him last week that I can't and won't give him a meal for free. That includes not giving him my employee discount, so he better be able to pay for whatever meal he orders today.

"Afternoon! I'll take a cheeseburger and fries." Oliver nods once I walk up to him.

"Do you plan on paying for your meal?"

"Wow! That's rude." He huffs a fake gasp as if he's truly offended.

"It's not rude when it's true." I remind him of his visit here last week and our argument about not allowing him to eat for free or at a discounted rate just because I work here.

"I've got the money, see?" He pulls out a twenty-dollar bill from his wallet. Just enough to cover the meal with a couple cents left over for my tip.

"Speaking of money, how's the job search going?"

"It's going."

"Have you applied anywhere lately?"

"What about here?"

"You've never worked as a server before. And trust me, you don't want to work here," I laugh.

"Can't be that hard."

"Wow, thanks for telling me my job is easy," I scoff. Although, he is right. Serving food can be easy except for the part where I have to deal with needy customers and petty coworkers. Memorizing the entire menu isn't such a breeze either.

"Hey, I didn't mean it like that."

"Sure you didn't. How do you want the burger cooked?"

"Well done. But seriously, do you think you can get me an interview here?"

"Why don't you just ask my manager yourself?"

"Okay, call her over here." He smirks.

Damnit, this man is agonizing. If he wants to screw with me, then fine. Time to call his bluff. I already know my manager will not ask him for an interview without a resume which I bet, Oliver isn't carrying on him. He has no interest in working here or anywhere for that matter.

I walk back to the kitchen to find Alana after putting Oliver's order through the POS system.

When we arrive back at Oliver's table, he looks up from his phone, eyes wide. I suppress a laugh.

"Uh, hello." He clears his throat. "Madison told me you might be hiring."

Liar.

"Do you have a resume with you?"

"I can email it to you right now."

My manager surprisingly gives him her contact info and to even more of my surprise, Oliver emails her his resume right from his phone. My other tables need my assistance so I tend to them while Oliver talks Alana's ear off.

He's smirking when I come back to his table a few minutes later. "Well, that went great."

"Did it?" I cross my arms at my torso.

"She told me after I'm done eating, I can sit with her for an official interview. She's going to look at my resume now. It seemed like I might get the job."

"Seriously?" Surprised at my own plan backfiring on me, my voice raises so much that the customers at the table behind him turn around to look at us.

He winks. "Looks like we're gonna get even closer than we've been getting lately."

"Great..."

I was only trying to mess with Oliver since he was clearly trying to mess with me. I shouldn't have brought Alana to meet him. Admittedly, I enjoy flirting with him sometimes, but working with him is not a good idea. He definitely needs a job. Just not the same one as mine.

"Hey, Danny thinks he lost his dad's ring last night so we're going back to the prison to look for it tonight. The man's worried. I feel bad. Want to come with us?"

As I am about to respond, a series of emergency alert notification sounds fill the diner. Everybody with a phone, including me and Oliver look at our screens.

TROPICAL STORM WATCH
***Tropical storm activity beginning tomorrow Sunday 10:00 p.m. until Monday 11:00 p.m.**
***Expect 50-60 mph winds**
***Rainfall 4-6 inches**

"Good thing the storm might not hit until tomorrow. Come with us tonight. It'll be fun. Plus, it'll be easier to search for the ring when there's more of us," he says, trying to convince me.

The thought of going back to an abandoned building sober makes me wince though. I shake my head and laugh. "Definitely not, but have fun. Hope you guys find it."

Had I known that I would inadvertently end up back at the prison (even though I said I wouldn't), and live the worst night of my life where I would witness a murder, I would have begged Oliver and Danny to not go back for the ring instead of telling them to have fun.

4

ERIC

SATURDAY - 11:30 p.m.

The perfect cure for a hangover is a good workout—especially two workouts in one day. I already went to the gym once this morning and now I'm back for a second time tonight.

Whether it's three or five o'clock in the morning—depending on what time the construction site needs me by, I come to the gym right before work throughout my weekdays. On the weekends, I come here twice; once in the morning and once at night.

On Saturday nights, Danny usually meets me here around eleven o'clock after he gets out of work, but he isn't here yet. He was supposed to meet me almost half an hour ago and it is not like him to be late. He has never once missed a session without good reason. Not when his arm was broken a couple of years ago, and not even the day after his dad died. In fact, he was right back at it, working out harder than ever the day after his dad passed. And can you blame him? Exercise is the best form of therapy in my opinion.

He hasn't replied to my text that I sent a few minutes ago and his phone went straight to voicemail the two times I called. I assumed he was on the other line or his phone died after work. Now I wonder if he's just not showing up because he's still hungover from last night. Or maybe, his dad's death has finally caught up to him and he doesn't want to be bothered. Maybe taking him out last night did the opposite of what we all wanted. Whatever the case, I'll give him a pass for being a no show tonight.

SUNDAY - 2:00 p.m.

It wasn't until I went back to the gym after I woke up this morning that I realized Danny hasn't texted or called me back yet. It's already two o'clock in the afternoon and he still hasn't responded or called. I'm not one to be a naggy wife, but something just feels off.

Since a tropical storm is going to hit us tonight, the roads in this town are going to be flooded for the next few days, regardless of how much rain the town is projected to get. These roads always flood out with heavy rain, so I have to get in a good run today because the gym will most likely be closed until the roads are clear.

On my way out of the door, I try calling Danny again.

Again, straight to voicemail.

Maybe he forgot to pay his bill. Oliver, the unemployed son of a bitch, should be home. He ain't got no money to spend anywhere or a job to be at today. I bet he's still sleeping.

Time to wake his ass up.

Or not. Straight to voicemail when I call his phone too.

Oliver's phone getting turned off for not paying the bill isn't something to worry about but this is too much of a coincidence that they both forgot to pay their bills. They are not on the same phone plan and Danny makes enough money to keep his phone on.

They hardly pay the same rent too. Danny told me Oliver is three months behind on his half of the rent. I don't know how or why he puts up with that bullshit. Two decades of friendship doesn't trump the bills.

When I hooked Oliver up at my job a few months ago (which is the last job he got fired from) I warned my boss about him. He's my best friend, but I was not about to let him be the reason I lost a job. He couldn't handle waking up early. I warned my boss so he wouldn't blame me for his lack of work ethic and thankfully, my boss understood when he fired Oliver after only two weeks.

Although his phone keeps going to voicemail, I still send Danny another text. ***You good, man?***

While awaiting a response, I try Oliver again.

Straight to voicemail, so I send him the same text I sent Danny.

They live a block away from me and since I'm already heading out on my run, I might as well make a pit stop and see what the hell's going on. On my way out of the door, a weather alert notification goes off on my phone.

TROPICAL STORM WARNING
***Tropical storm activity beginning tonight Sunday 10:00 p.m. until Monday 11:00 p.m.**
***Expect 50-60 mph winds**
***Rainfall 4-6 inches**

As if on cue, a dead palm tree leaf falls off a tree in the wind outside when I open my door.

With the breeze flowing through my hair while running over to their apartment, my mind oddly begins filling with paranoid thoughts. What if something happened to their apartment and that's why they're not answering? A gas leak maybe? A fire?

Well, shit. I think I'm turning into my sister by thinking so negatively. Is this how

Maddie's brain works? Always in a state of constant worry. Constant pessimistic thoughts running through her mind— always thinking the worst situation possible.

Hell, that's exhausting. I love my little sister but I don't want to think like her.

Minutes later, when Danny and Oliver's two-story apartment building comes into view, I notice that nothing seems out of the ordinary. Doesn't seem like the residents got evacuated either. No flames spewing from the building. No firetrucks or emergency vehicles anywhere. Two people just walked into separate apartments on the first and second floor. There are a few people sitting outside on their balconies. Danny's truck isn't parked anywhere in the small parking lot though.

On the first floor, I round the corner to reach their doorstep. Oliver's bike is outside of the door so he should be home. He never walks anywhere unless he's in the truck with Danny.

I knock three times on their door and call out, "Aye fuckfaces! Answer the door. It's me!"

No response. There's no sound coming from inside of the apartment at all. I don't hear the TV on. No voices in conversation. I jiggle the door to find it locked. "Danny! Oliver!"

Still no answer. As I'm turning around to leave, I trip over their doormat and I remember Oliver telling me he leaves a spare key underneath. I push the doormat up with my sneaker. A shiny silver key sits beneath it.

After inserting the key and opening the door, I step into a silent apartment— too silent. Oliver and Danny aren't anywhere in here. They aren't in their bedrooms. Nobody is in the bathroom. I don't see their phones or wallets laying out on the kitchen counter or table...

Then where the hell are they?

My alarm on my phone goes off, telling me it's three o'clock— time to go pick up Maddie from work. Since her car broke down last week and has been in the shop ever since, I have unfortunately become her chauffeur.

Before leaving their apartment, I call Danny and Oliver's phones one more time. Again, both phones go straight to voicemail and I didn't hear a phone ringing here in the apartment either.

After helping myself to a water bottle from their fridge, I lock the door to their apartment behind me and take the key with me, so I can run back home to jump in my car to pick up my sister.

About twenty-five minutes later, Maddie gets in the passenger side, reeking of a combination of pancakes, eggs, burgers and fries.

"How was work?" I mockingly question her in the same way our father would ask about school when we were kids.

"Same as always. It was better than yesterday at least. Working with a hangover during morning shift sucks. Today wasn't as bad because I wasn't hungover this time."

My phone rings and quicker than I expected, I grab it from the cup holder, hoping it's either Danny or Oliver calling me back.

Spam likely instead.

"You alright?" Maddie raises her eyebrows.

"Yeah. I've been trying to call Danny since last night. He never showed up to the gym. Both his and Oliver's phones keep going to voicemail and I went to their apartment before I picked you up just now. They weren't there. I think somethings wrong, but I'm not sure what's going on."

"Oh, really?" Madison looks down at her phone. "When was the last time you heard from either of them?"

"When we all went out for drinks the other night."

"Oh..." she mumbles. Her tone sounds of worry.

"What's wrong? What do you know that I don't?"

"Well, Oliver told me that he was going back to the prison last night with Danny to look for his dad's ring. I guess Danny lost it when we were there the night before."

"What ring?"

"Danny's father's ring!" she exclaims, but the rise in her tone doesn't halt my confusion until she reminds me that Danny's dad gave him his college ring a few hours before his spleen ruptured— a delayed reaction from the car accident, which inevitably caused him to die.

"What a great friend you are," Maddie sighs. "How did you forget that?"

"Hey, men are different than women are. We don't remember details like y'all do. It's not because I don't care. It just slipped my mind."

While turning into the parking lot of her apartment complex, I realize what she just said. Since when has she become so friendly with Oliver? They never hang out or talk to each other unless they're with me. "Wait, when did you talk to Oliver?"

"Uhm, yesterday. He came by the diner before I got off my shift."

"Why?" Oliver's been my best friend since high school, but that doesn't mean I trust him with my sister.

"I guess he wanted free food."

I would believe Maddie if she actually looked me in the face just now. She normally tells me everything. Right now, she isn't though. I can tell that she is uncomfortable, so I won't press for more information. If something is going on between them, then it ain't my business. Madison can make her own decisions. Oliver can be dimwitted but he should know better than to fuck with my sister.

"So have you heard from him after he was at the diner yesterday?" I ask while she opens the passenger side door.

"Nope. That was the last I saw and heard from him." Before getting out of the car, she turns to me. "Have you checked their Instagram's to see if they posted or been on there today? I haven't had time at work to scroll."

Shaking my head, I scroll over to both of their profiles which only further confirms my worries. There aren't any recent posts or stories on either Danny or Oliver's profiles other than the picture that Oliver posted of us the night we went to the prison.

"Oliver should probably delete evidence of us breaking the law," Madison says while looking at her phone as she views his profile herself. "I look terrible in this picture. Try calling Lucas. Maybe he's heard from them today."

"Good idea." I set the phone on speaker when Lucas answers after a couple rings. He sounds half asleep.

"You're still sleeping, man?" I laugh.

"I was just napping. I ran errands this morning then went back to sleep," he groggily says.

Lucas has been a bit depressed lately because of his divorce and childcare situation. His ex-wife insists that his kid goes to day care on the weekends when Lucas rather have him home since he doesn't even work on the weekends. I don't blame him. If I were in his situation, I would be mad too.

"Have you heard from Oliver or Danny today?"

"No," he groans, half asleep.

I tell him I'll call him later and end the call.

"Well, this doesn't sound good." Madison sits back against the passenger seat with one foot out of the door. "What should we do?"

"Not sure. Am I being paranoid about this? Danny's truck wasn't in the parking lot at their apartment, but Oliver's bike was outside of the door. So then, they must still be together."

"Maybe we should call the police to report them missing," she suggests except that doesn't sound as straightforward as she wants it to be.

"And tell the police that our friends went missing when they had plans to go trespass last night? Yeah, that's a terrific idea. They'll ask us where they were going before and why they went there."

She sighs. "I guess you're right. And that would be pretty embarrassing—admitting to the cops that a group of thirty-year-olds broke into an abandoned building while we were drunk."

"Well, you have to admit, it was a fun night."

"Was it? I really can't remember much of it. I hardly remember leaving the bar."

"Maybe we should go to the prison and look for them then," I suggest. "If we call the cops, I doubt they'll go looking for them at the prison anyway. They're adults. I don't think the police will take us seriously."

Although, my idea does not sound so great either. Exploring the place the other night was a good idea at the time because of the alcohol, but going back without it seems like a bad idea. Actually, it's probably just as bad of an idea as it was when we were intoxicated. Except this time, we would be going back for Oliver and Danny, so maybe it's not such a bad idea after all.

"If they're still at the prison, then that would not be a good sign," she says.

Here goes my sister with the pessimism.

"Before we break the law again, try calling Lucas back. Ask him to talk to Amy. See if she's heard from Oliver today. If she hasn't, then I guess we'll have to go back to look for them."

My sister can be a bit cynical, but I admit she is also pretty smart too. Calling Lucas back to talk to Amy first is actually a better idea than downright going on a manhunt at the prison first.

Lucas has Amy's number because they share a day care for their kids. There have been times when they carpooled (against Lucas's wishes because he is not a fan of Amy, as none of us are).

"Call me when you know what's going on." Maddie abruptly gets out of my car.

As I text Lucas, that nagging feeling of something being wrong weighs over me.

How does that saying go? When you feel something is wrong, then normally it is?

Well, man did I feel something was off which is what led me, my sister and Lucas all back to the prison.

Always follow your intuition— That's how the saying goes.

Shit, I'm glad I did follow my instincts. I just wish I didn't wait so long to act upon them.

5

L U C A S

SUNDAY - 4:00 p.m.

Holding onto a secret while being drunk takes a lot of self-control. I'm surprised I didn't blurt anything out when I was with my friends the other night at the bar and the prison.

If only they knew where I was a few days before we went out, they would have shit themselves knowing I willingly went out drinking and trespassed with them. Especially Maddie. She would have scolded me about how much of a risk I was taking.

And she would be right. Drinking wasn't much of a risk because none of us were driving, but it was risky for me to break the law again when we broke into the prison. But in the end, the risk outweighed the cost because there was no cost. It was actually a fun night— a fun forgetful night, nevertheless an adventure.

I slightly recall talking to Eric in my sleep a few minutes ago. Why was he asking about Oliver and Danny? He called me right after I started my nap to get rid of my raging headache once I got back home this morning from running a few errands.

Ding.

Ding.

Ding.

Three text messages shine brightly on my screen as I sit up in bed. Waking up to several messages from the mother of my child reminding me to pick our son up from day care in an hour is not what I want to see during this hangover. The nap helped a bit, but not entirely.

Before divorcing, we were together for six years. Only four months ago, shortly after our son turned five, she decided living a life without me would be better for her in the long run; Her words exactly.

Since I did not have my son last night, I drank myself to a near coma and I shouldn't have because I did the same thing the night before at the bar with my friends. I only went to help out Danny. Oliver's suggestion to explore the prison actually added on to distracting Danny from the harsh realities of his life. Yeah, it was a bit childish, at our ages to break into a building in the middle of the night. I'm just glad we didn't get arrested, despite how much of a risk I was taking. It felt like we were teenagers again—carefree, trespassing in places we had no business being in. No regrets there.

The only regret I have is drinking an entire twenty-four pack of beer last night by myself. Although my head is pounding, I'm fully sober now (the day nap helped) as I get ready to go pick up my son from day care— a day care that is not needed because I am off work on the weekends. My ex-wife, on the other hand, thinks otherwise. Since we paid the day care three months in advance before we settled our divorce, she believes we need to get our money's worth. Hence the reason I drank last night.

Sitting in an empty house alone is depressing as a single father, especially when I remind myself that a group of strangers are babysitting my own son. Meanwhile I am fully capable and available to keep him home with me. If I could have spent the day with my son today, I wouldn't have drank by myself at all last night. Same as the night before. I wouldn't have gone out with my friends to the bar and prison either.

After swiping away from my ex-wife's messages, a new text from Eric appears on my phone. He wants me to talk to Amy to see if she's heard from Oliver. Now that I am fully awake and functioning, I text him back to see what's going on.

While on my way to the day care that is stealing all of my money and aiding to my depression, I give Oliver a call first. Despite Eric telling me that Oliver and Danny haven't answered their phones since last night, I want to try calling myself.

Straight to voicemail.

I try calling Danny.

Voicemail too.

As soon as I hang up, my phone rings.

MOM CALLING.

Ignore.

Never in my life did I think I'd find myself divorced and my parents sure as hell don't want to hear that, which is why they don't know about anything yet. They loved my ex-wife. Sometimes it seems like they love her more than me. They definitely love my son more than the both of us. That's undeniable.

Twenty minutes later, Amy's already inside of the day care when I arrive. It's too noisy in here to strike up a conversation so I'll wait until we're in the parking lot. Not that I want to actually talk to her, but I'll do it for Danny and Oliver.

Amy's son came from a relationship before she and Oliver started dating which is one of the main reasons why they can't be together. Oliver is not father material, let alone able to be a stepdad. He denies it when we all know it's true. My best friend's a good guy, just not a responsible one.

"Hey, Amy!" I call out to her as she approaches her car once we're free from all the noise inside the day care.

The wind is starting to pick up from the approaching hurricane that is set to hit the other side of the coast, which will bring us tropical storm weather later tonight. It isn't raining yet, but by the looks of the sky, I expect it to start downpouring soon.

"Daddy! I wanna go home! I'm hungry," my son whines at my side while clinging onto my pants.

Three hundred dollars a week and the babysitters can't even provide him a proper meal. Typical.

"Just give me a few minutes. We'll get food on the way home," I say as we walk up to Amy. "Hey! Amy! Wait a second!"

Either it's me or the wind that startles her because she jumps at the sound of her name. Her car door closes before she tries to get in, nearly slamming her fingers in between.

"DAMNIT!" She turns around with creased eyebrows.

She reminds me of the models on those ads for the before picture of women before they get Botox. I wonder what it's like to always be as anxiety ridden and angry as she is.

Actually, no I don't want to know what that's like at all. I'm already depressed and that is becoming almost unmanageable. Anxiety isn't a symptom I want to add on to depression.

"You heard from Oliver lately?" I ask.

"Nope, not today." She nods down at my wrist. "Looks like we're matching." She flashes a yellow and blue beaded bracelet wrapped around her own wrist— the same bracelet my son just gave me in the day care.

"Our sons are so creative," I smile. I guess it was arts and crafts day today. Both of our bracelets are identical, yellow and blue beads decorated with the letter I, a heart, and a U. "When was the last time you heard from Oliver?"

"Oh, last night when we had dinner. We went to eat and then he came over for a little bit after..." She directs her eyesight at her son and mine, telepathically telling me what he came over for without verbalizing it. *Figures.* "Then he left to go meet Danny. He said they were going back to that pris— that place y'all went to the other night." She clears her throat, exchanging another look to both of our sons.

Amy may be a bit ditzy, but at least she is not ditzy enough to bring up the words *sex* and *prison* in front of our five-year-olds.

"What time did he leave your place?"

"He left a little before ten. He told me they were going back to look for a ring or something. I haven't heard from him since then."

"Alright, thanks."

"Bye Taylor!" My son waves at her son who does not look as happy as my son is to be leaving day care. I don't think Amy is an abusive parent but the look on Taylor's face tells the same as an abused kid who hates going home.

As we are about to part ways, a notification blares on both of our phones.

TROPICAL STORM WATCH IN EFFECT.

10:00 p.m. tonight Sunday until 11:00 p.m. Monday

*Locations affected: EVERGLADES CITY, FL

-LATEST LOCAL FORCAST:

*Expect tropical storm force winds

-Peak wind forecast: 55 mph with up to-60 mph wind gusts

-Expect 4-6 inches of rain

"Great. My brakes are bad in my car, and there's a hole in my ceiling at home too. I better get home before the rain comes. Then I have to take Taylor to his dad's tonight because the idiot refuses to come pick him up. I hate hurricane season!" I faintly hear

Amy complaining to nobody because I am already walking away from her.

"Daddy, Taylor told me he doesn't like his mom. All she does is yell at him and get mad at everything and he says, his dad doesn't do that. His dad plays video games with him like you do with me and they make forts in the backyard. He says he doesn't like living with his mom. He was really happy to go to his dad's tonight."

I'm sure he was. I don't blame him.

As much as I wish I could stay home tonight with my son, a tropical storm will not convince my ex-wife that my son should stay with me tonight because she is already expecting for him to spend the night at her house. Hell, she probably thinks he'll be safer with her anyways. No room to argue with her since it looks like I'll be heading back to the prison with Eric and Maddie tonight.

Regardless of my situation, I can't let Eric and Maddie go back there without me anyway. I'm worried about Oliver and Danny now. Nobody is going to look for them besides us. They're adults. I'm pretty sure the police won't put out a missing person search after only a few hours.

I text Eric. *Amy hasn't heard from him. Dropping my son off at 8:00 tonight. Meet at your place after?*

Danny's been super depressed since his dad died which is expected. I know what losing someone close is like— not in the parental losing aspect, but I know what it's like to lose a loved one. When my uncle died last year from a sudden heart attack, my world changed. The man was like a second father to me. He was in my life from the moment I was born.

I still have moments of sadness, grief, anger—all the emotions you expect to have when losing someone close to you. Time doesn't change anything. Whether it's two days, two weeks or twenty years later, the pain still sits with you forever.

Danny has no family except us now. If we don't look for him, nobody will.

Had I known that returning to the prison a second time would put us all in even greater danger than we were in the first time, I would have insisted we reported Danny and Oliver missing and hoped that the police would handle it.

Then again, if we hadn't shown up when we did, I'm not sure anyone would have come out of the prison alive either.

6

MADISON

SUNDAY - 9:15 p.m.

I was wrong when I said sober me would never explore an abandoned building because here I am, sitting in the passenger seat of Eric's car in front of an abandoned prison at nine o'clock at night again. This time, I am soberly aware of my actions and surroundings.

The dense mangroves, towering cypress trees, and murky water, along with the ominous night sky, howling wind, the scent of the rain, and thunder adds to my unease.

It's very unlike Danny to skip the gym especially without contacting Eric. It is also very unlike Eric to be even slightly concerned about anything. If it weren't for how recent and sudden the death of Danny's father was, none of us would be this concerned about Danny not answering right now.

I am not a true crime junkie, but I have watched enough of those documentaries and thriller movies that my brain has been altered to assume something bad must have happened to my friends when they were either on their way to the prison last night, or after they left. Or something could have even happened when they were inside looking for the ring. Maybe they had an accident of some kind and can't get to their phones.

As Eric shifts his BMW into park on the two-lane road that is in desperate need for repaving outside of the prison, an eerie but familiar feeling that I can't pinpoint creeps upon me. I said I never want to get as drunk as I did the other night, but again, I was very wrong. A shot or two right now would not be such a bad idea. It would at least calm my nerves.

We haven't even stepped foot on the property yet and I already feel creeped out. Also, a bit ridiculous. At twenty-nine years old, I shouldn't be here. Neither should my thirty-one-year-old friends and brother. Neither sober or drunk.

Even though lightning illuminates the sky and thunder crashes in the distance, it still somehow feels eerily quiet out here. This desolate stretch of road links to the more residential part of Everglades City, yet few cars ever pass through here. Half-paved and half-dirt filled, this road serves as a backroad for locals looking to bypass the main streets, shrouded in an unsettling stillness. The nearest business is the bar that we went to the other night which is in a residential area.

Standing here now in the dead of the night, I wonder how we walked two entire miles on a dark road as drunk as we were. We know better than to stroll along the Everglades at night. Our inebriated selves, on the other hand, did not.

Because we were so inebriated, the walk here and back to the bar is absent from my memory. For all I know, we could have been chased by a coyote, or worse— an alligator, and just simply had good luck that the wildlife out here didn't decide to have us for dinner.

People always talk about feeling superhuman and invincible while being drunk. Turns out, they were right.

I immediately notice that Eric's car is the only vehicle parked on the road in front of the prison. Danny's truck should be here too if they're still inside of the building. That is, if he and Oliver even made it back here last night. Like I said, something could have happened on the way here... or on the way back home.

"Well, Danny's truck isn't out here," I say.

"Wrong. Danny's truck's right there!" Lucas points over in the direction of the prison as he begins walking ahead of us.

From where I was just standing outside of the driver side of Eric's car near the backseat, I didn't notice the dirt road on the side of the building around the left corner, until I start to follow Lucas.

As Eric and I trail behind him along the ten-foot-tall barbwire fence that surrounds the property, Danny's truck comes into my sight. A cold shiver runs through my spine. Seeing Danny's truck only heightens my anxiety.

"Well, this is a good sign so far. At least we found his truck," says Lucas.

"No, it isn't a good sign," I argue.

I turn around to make sure nobody's watching us. Although, even if a vehicle drove by, they wouldn't see us on this side of the fence. They won't even see Danny's truck and that is probably why he parked it over here. But they will see Eric's car instead because he parked right in front of the building. I think twice about telling him to move it. He'll just tell me I'm being paranoid and nobody will care that we're here.

And he would be right. Nobody *should* care that we're out here. I know we are the only people in the area, but why does it feel like somebody is watching us?

Then again, I guess someone watching isn't an entire impossibility.

Anyone could be hiding in between the trees. That is, if someone is brave enough to hide out amongst the alligators and whatever other threatening wildlife the Everglades is home to. But this is Florida after all. The stereotypical joke that *Florida man* exists is very much a real stereotype for a reason. I shouldn't be skeptical of somebody hiding out around here at all.

As we approach Danny's truck, neither he or Oliver are inside. The rest of the dirt road that his truck is parked on ends only a few feet past the prison and into the woods. The road must've been utilized only for the prison before the building partially burned down.

Lucas plasters his face against the window on the truck even though the windows are not tinted and we can see inside of the vehicle perfectly. He attempts to pull open the door handle on the driver side. Clearly, all doors are locked and the engine isn't running. I don't see the keys in the ignition, anywhere on the seats or out in the open either. Their cell phones and wallets aren't even here. At least, not anywhere that we can see of.

"They must still be inside the prison then," Lucas says.

That unnerving feeling is getting stronger within me. *Again, this is not a good sign that something isn't wrong with our friends. This is a bad sign. Very bad.*

If Danny and Oliver are okay, then they would have made it home by now. They would have answered us at one point. Why would they still be inside of the prison with their phones turned off?

Probably because they can't answer for a reason. And not a good reason. Everything about this situation is raising red flags. I want to report them missing but I fear the police won't actually do anything.

I mean, what would they do anyways? Come here to the prison and look for them, then find them, and eventually arrest them for trespassing? Along with us too? Should we be worried about getting arrested outweighing the risk that something could be very wrong?

Then again, we're already here. Might as well look for them before involving police.

"This place is a lot bigger than I remember it being the other night," Eric says as he turns to look at the building.

Even though we have all driven by this building many times before and after it caught on fire several years ago, I do not recall this place looking so big and ominous. Maybe it's just my nerves or that familiar unsettling feeling that I can't pinpoint.

"This whole area is a lot darker out here than I remember it was the other night too," I say.

I just noticed there aren't any streetlights around here or any light around the building at all.

But of course, there aren't any streetlights or lights on the building because this place has been abandoned for years now.

Seven years ago, a fire destroyed half of the prison, along with over fifty of the inmates inside. And as we walk up to the fence right now, I begin thinking about the possibility of the spirits of the inmates being here. Not that I am one to believe in ghosts, but this *is* a place where people actually died. I am sure there is some form of the afterlife roaming around here.

Maybe that's the eerie feeling I'm getting. Almost as if someone is watching us.

Or maybe hanging out with the guys after all these years really has dumbed me down.

Sure, spirits could be lingering around here but this is not a horror movie. The afterlife isn't malicious. Spirits are not the culprit of what's happened to my friends. Not that I want something bad to have happened to them, except the odds of the scenario are not looking to be in our favor so far.

As we walk away from Danny's truck, the closer we get to the fence, the unsettling feeling of being watched grows stronger.

Is it Florida man hiding out amongst the trees and living up to the typical stereotype?

Or is my subconscious telling me my friends are truly in danger?

Out of the two choices, I hope it's Florida man.

7

MADISON

SUNDAY - 9:30 p.m.

Eric shines the flashlight on his phone alongside the chain link fence over a hole that has already been cut by someone other than ourselves. At least, I think someone else cut through the fence. If it was anyone in our group the other night, I have no memory of who it was or how we did it.

Eric and Lucas bend down to crawl through the hole. While Eric has a harder time getting through without getting scraped from the fence because he is bigger muscle wise, Lucas and I easily fit without a problem.

Once again, I look around the area to see if anyone is watching us. The absence of people and vehicles out here makes me feel only somewhat at ease. (Emphasis on somewhat.)

At the front entrance of the prison, we're greeted by a large sign— Blackridge Penitentiary and a rusted old pad lock that needs a code to get the front door unlocked. The lock was probably put on by the city after the building shut down.

"Well, unless we figured out the code the other night, this can't be the way we got into the building before," Lucas says. He attempts to yank open the lock by pulling at it. The lock is obviously old, but it's clearly not broken because it won't budge off the doorknob. Even with the proper code, I wonder if the thing even opens anymore.

There are two windows that aren't broken or boarded up by plywood next to the door. Eric attempts to lift open both windows but of course, they don't budge.

"I'm going to look for a way in on the other side," he says and goes over to the side of the building that did not burn in the fire.

Lucas remains stumped at the front entrance as he continues to try to yank the lock off the door while I venture over to the side of the building that caught on fire. Although part of this building fell victim to a fire, the front and left side of the prison is almost perfectly intact. Plywood panels have been used to board up the windows. Broken yellow caution tape hangs loosely around the building. After all these years, I'm surprised the tape hasn't been torn off completely.

"We must've gone in through one of the gaps in the plywood," says Lucas when he comes up next to me, surveying the area with his phone's flashlight.

Thinking about it now, he might be right. Pain and getting dirty are not such a concern when you are drunk. Thinking logically is clearly not present either.

I spot a gap on the bottom of the plywood that looks just large enough for me to squeeze through. Oliver and Lucas can probably fit through without a problem too. I can't see Eric or Danny getting through because they're more muscular than the rest of us. Then this can't be the way that we all got into the building last time.

"Maddie! Lucas!" Eric yells. "I found another door over here."

We follow my brother's voice to find him standing in front of a black door on the other side of the building. He shines his phone's flashlight at the handle which does not have a padlock on it. He turns the handle freely, looks at us and shrugs before opening the door all the way. He points his phone's flashlight ahead before walking in the building.

Why is the front entrance padlocked only, and not the side entrance? Unless there was a padlock on the door at one point and teenagers broke it off.

Or maybe it was us who broke off the lock the other night when we initially broke in.

"Well, this is better than crawling through the other side. Now I won't get dirt all over my clothes," Lucas huffs.

Of course he was concerned about getting his outfit dirty. Even though he knew where we were going tonight, he still chose to wear a designer white T-shirt, expensive jeans, and brand-new bright yellow sneakers. Does he think he's matching or was his eccentric outfit choice for the night on purpose?

I've never understood his logic and never will. Lucas and Oliver are basically the same person, except Lucas has a firmer grip on his life. He's also not as lackadaisical when it comes to responsibilities as Oliver is. I believe his son is the reason he keeps his life on the right track. That said, he's still just as lacking in common sense as Oliver is. Having common sense can't really be changed but at least his priorities remain on the right track.

As I follow Eric through the side entrance of the prison, the unsettling feeling that hit me outside of the fence is growing stronger.

It's my nerves. I'm just anxious.

I'm worried about Danny and Oliver.

I'm also worried about getting arrested for trespassing.

That's all it is.

And of course I'm anxious tonight.

I'm fully sober. I know we are here to strictly find our friends, but we wouldn't be lurking around this place if we didn't decide to act like teenagers a few nights before. The alcohol played a huge role in our decision and now we're all facing the consequences.

As we enter the building, I audibly gasp when all three of our phones each blare with an emergency alert from the national weather service. If I weren't so nervous, the alert would not have almost given me a slight heart attack either.

TROPICAL STORM WARNING IN EFFECT

*Now until Monday 11:00 p.m.

HAZARD... *Wind gusts up to 55-60 mph*

*Flooding of small creaks, rivers, and waterways. *

*Expect 6-8 inches of rain.

As if on cue, the rain suddenly picks up to a downpour and the lightning commences outside right as we close the door behind us.

I think we shouldn't have come here.

8

MADISON

SUNDAY - 10:00 p.m.

Now that we are inside of the building, I do slightly recall entering through this side entrance the other night.

Okay, I don't *actually* remember walking in through here, but this dark hallway does look familiar to me in the ray of our phone's flashlights. A row of inmate holding cells align the left side of the hallway. On the right side of the hallway, old graffiti decorates the off-white wall. As I expected, there is absolutely no light in here and since we're relying on our phones, I have a hunch to check my battery.

Seventy one percent.

As long as we don't spend a long time in here, then my phone should stay on long enough until we find our friends.

"How much battery do you guys have on your phones?" I ask.

"Sixty-seven," Eric answers.

"Fifty-eight," says Lucas.

I exasperatedly sigh, wishing they would have said their phones are at least charged to over seventy percent like mine is. I guess sixty-seven and fifty-eight are better than twenty percent or ten percent though.

"We'll be fine, Maddie. We're not going to be here that long," Eric tries to reassure me.

Let's hope not.

As we head down the hallway, I point my light into one of the cells. A single cot bed with an off-white bedsheet (now a tan yellowish color from aging) sits against the wall next to a disgusting urinal.

"Creepy," Lucas mutters when he shines his flashlight into another cell. A handful of faded drawings lay out on the floor and three dolls eerily sit on the bed.

Well, that's a little odd to find in a prison. I wonder if the dolls were gifts to the inmates before this place shut down or if some teenagers who trespassed like us, brought the dolls here. Or maybe the dolls belonged to a homeless person. Possibly a runaway kid even. After all, this building has been abandoned for years now. It's obvious we aren't the only ones to explore this place because of all the graffiti in here.

After passing twelve cells (and no sign of our friends in any of them), we are faced with the option to only turn right when we reach the end of the hallway.

As we round the corner, Eric nearly trips over a wheelchair. The memory of Lucas and Oliver pushing Danny around the hallway reappears in my brain.

"Remember this?" I point out the wheelchair to Lucas. "Y'all were pushing each other up and down this hallway in this wheelchair..."

"Ah, yeah! Now the night is starting to come back to me," Lucas laughs.

After following the path of the hallway, we led ourselves right to the lobby where the door to the front entrance outside is padlocked. ISITOR WAITING AREA is sprawled across the wall with the letter V missing on the sign when we walk out into the open space. A couple of chairs are flipped over while some lay on their sides, creating a chaotic maze for us to carefully navigate around. Broken glass that once enclosed an old desk sits in the middle of the room.

On the left side of the area, I spot another room. The door is broken off from the hinges. I walk inside to find a couple of phones attached to the booths, or more so, unattached and just dangling by the cords.

The glass in between the inmate and visitor sections is shattered. Behind the broken glass, three doors are closed. I assume the inmates came out from behind those doors to see their visitors. There must be another hallway that leads back to more cells through there.

This place is a huge maze and the more we explore, the more I realize it's going to take us longer to search this place than we intended. So far, there is no sign of Danny and Oliver anywhere. I don't see the keys to Danny's truck anywhere. Their phones aren't laying around either.

"Seems like teenagers trashed this place, huh?" Lucas laughs when I walk back into the lobby which prompts me to remember I recorded a video of us in here.

"Yeah, we were the teenagers who trashed it. We threw these chairs around. I remember throwing them at each other," Eric says.

A video on my phone confirms he is right. Oliver, Lucas, Eric and Danny are the reason why all these chairs are on the ground. While stumbling, they hysterically laughed as they threw the chairs at each other like they were playing a game of dodgeball. I guess I thought it was funny too because you can hear me hilariously laughing as I recorded them.

"Danny! Oliver!" Suddenly Eric shouts and nearly sends me into a panic.

"Shh!" I smack his arm because we are not supposed to be here. Making noise in a place we're trespassing in is not a smart idea. "We shouldn't make so much noise!"

"What's the problem?" Eric shrugs. "This place is huge. If Danny and Oliver are still in here, how else do you plan on finding them? We have to call their names, at least. We can't just walk around aimlessly hoping to run into them."

"We shouldn't be yelling though. Someone could hear us and call the police on us."

"Who would hear us?" Eric huffs. "Nobody's in here besides us and hopefully, Danny and Oliver. I'm sure we made a shit load of noise the other night when we were trashed. If no one heard us then, nobody is going to hear us now. And nobody's going to hear us with all the rain and thunder outside anyways. Relax."

"Danny! Oliver!" Lucas shouts.

The rain batters against the two large windows that are not boarded up by plywood near the front door. Thunder crashes, causing me to flinch.

"Let's just split up. We shouldn't—" I stop myself from finishing my sentence.

Wait a second. Maybe *I actually have* lost some common sense hanging around my brother and male friends after all these years. I am so worried about us getting arrested for trespassing here when I haven't thought of the same possibility for Danny and Oliver. Sighing, I'm upset that I forwent rational thinking before agreeing to come back here tonight.

On my phone, I search for the latest mugshots from our local police station. If Oliver and Danny got caught snooping around here last night, like we're looking for them right now, then they could be held up in a jail cell. I wouldn't expect either of them to give us a call to bail them out because I'm sure none of our phone numbers are engraved in their memories. Oliver would never call his parents because they think he is a perfect angel and Danny has nobody to call besides us. Meanwhile, here we are roaming around this place with a possibility of landing ourselves in a cell with them.

"What are you doing?" Eric questions me as I look through the arrest records but unfortunately, my idea is shot down immediately. I can't find a mugshot of either Danny or Oliver or any arrest record for them at all. Not that I hoped they got arrested but if they did, then we would know where the hell they are and that they are safe at least.

"Never mind. I thought they might've gotten arrested for trespassing. They didn't."

"I don't think they would be in jail for trespassing, Maddie. They'd probably have to pay a fine but I doubt trespassing would land a person in jail," Eric says.

"Well, that's good they ain't arrested," Lucas says.

"Unless they're in a hospital instead," I think out loud. Since they aren't in jail, maybe they were in some type of accident as I originally thought, and they needed an ambulance. That would explain why their phones are both going to voicemail. Maybe they don't have a charger with them in the hospital.

"Why would they be in a hospital?" Lucas asks.

Clearly, my brother and Lucas live in a world where they choose to believe bad things don't happen to the people they love. I accept the fact that bad stuff can happen to everybody. No matter who the person is. It's called thinking realistically.

"Anything could have happened to them here, guys. Maybe they were in an accident and they had to call an ambulance or something. Maybe one of them fell."

There are no hospitals in town but there are a few just on the outskirts, roughly twenty to thirty minutes away, so Eric and I start to make some calls. Meanwhile, Lucas tries calling Danny and Oliver a few times.

But after speaking to the nearest hospitals, Eric and I are both told that neither Danny or Oliver have checked into or were brought into the emergency room within the past forty-eight hours.

"Okay, well this is getting to be worrisome," I mutter.

"I bet you're worried," Eric scoffs.

I ignore his little sly comment. It's obvious he is not happy that Oliver and I are suddenly closer than he is used to seeing us be. I know my brother does not want to pry into my personal life, except I know that he knows something is going on. But what he doesn't know is that Oliver is the one who started making sudden unannounced appearances at my job recently.

Although I admit flirting with Oliver is amusing, I prefer that he leaves me alone because I do not want to be in the middle of a toxic love triangle, especially with his psycho girlfriend/ex-girlfriend— whatever she is to him. Amy does not like me and she never will. And she most definitely won't like me once she finds out her man has been flirting with me.

"DANNY! OLIVER!" Lucas yells, although shouting their names is useless. The storm isn't lightening up. The loud rain and booming thunder mask his yells.

"They probably just can't hear us from here," Eric says.

"Or something bad happened and that's why they aren't answering us. They could be unconscious," I sigh.

"Why would they be unconscious?" Lucas shines the light from his phone at my face.

"Because like I said, they could have fallen or something. Are you guys not thinking about the real possibility that something could be seriously wrong?"

It seems like I am the only one who has thought of a harsher reality than what my brother and Lucas are expecting. Nothing about this night implicates our friends are fine. Especially since Danny's truck is still outside and their phones have been going straight to voicemail for an entire day now.

"You're just paranoid for no reason," Lucas scoffs before he shouts their names again.

"Let's just split up to look for them then. If we're going to call their names, we might as well not stand in one spot and do it," I reluctantly suggest. I hate that idea, but I'm not trying to spend the whole night here. If we split up, chances are we'll find them quicker.

"Is that a good idea— to split up?" Lucas scratches his head, apprehension in his expression.

His sudden objection makes me laugh. "Are you scared?"

But he ignores my question and calls their names again. A strike of lightning rumbles the building, furthering my point that the quicker we find them, the faster we'll get home and out of this storm.

"Maddie, I'm not letting you walk around here by yourself. Me and you will go look around the burned side of the building," Eric says, then gestures to Lucas. "You should go back down the other way we came in from. There's got to be a staircase somewhere to get to the second floor. Find it and we'll meet you over there."

"Sure, let me go off by myself. Thanks, bro," Lucas sighs.

We all head back out into the hallway that led us to the lobby and part ways. Eric and I turn right while Lucas goes left to head back toward the hallway where the side entrance of the building is.

We reach a few steps into the charred hallway walls, leaving only remnants of a few inmate cells on this floor and a staircase that does not look safe to stand on up ahead.

"We are not going on those stairs," I say.

"That's why I told Lucas to look for them on the other side. I'm sure there's more than one staircase in this place. DANNY! OLIVER? Y'all in here?" Eric yells.

No response.

"I found something," says Lucas when he suddenly comes up behind us.

I slightly flinch at his appearance when I hear his voice. We barely made it ten feet away from him before he got too scared to roam around without us.

"I found a door that we passed by and didn't look in. It leads to a shitload of more cells and another staircase," he says. "It's literally down the hall from here."

Without arguing, we turn around to follow him, passing the entrance to the main lobby. He takes us through a door that we passed earlier but didn't go in. I assumed it was just another cell, but I was wrong.

Well, sort of. Through here, we enter into a large area double the size of the main lobby. A small security room with broken TV's and computer monitors catches my eye before seeing a staircase that leads to the second floor which is shaped in a circular hallway. Rows of inmate cells align the top and bottom floors.

I shine my phone's flashlight around the first floor near the security room when I notice my name is written on the wall next to a door with the sign—MEDICAL CENTER above it.

"Wait... I wrote that?" I walk over toward the black ink, the light from my phone shining across the letters.

Yeah, that is definitely my handwriting—drunken handwriting. And it is my name. Even more shockingly, in the ray of my light, *Maddie* is written three more times down the wall just past the medical room. *What the hell is wrong with me?*

"Oh yeah!" laughs Lucas. "I remember you doing that! You had a sharpie in your purse and started writing your name everywhere. I got a video of you."

A video on Lucas's phone further confirms my drunkenly actions. There I am, stumbling with a sharpie, strewing my hand across the wall. Danny is pointing his phone's flashlight at the wall for me as I write my name while Oliver records me with his phone. Lucas captured the whole thing with his own phone from a few feet away.

"Wait a second..." I point my flashlight at the floor beneath my name. Since we know we were here last time because of my name, it's a possibility Danny could have dropped the ring around the area. "We should look for Danny's ring while we're looking for them too. If we find the ring, then that might mean they never even got this far into the building."

"We can also look at our phones from that night and see if the ring is on Danny's finger in any of the pictures or videos. Then we can figure out where to look around the building for it... and them, I guess," suggests Lucas which I admit, sounds like good detective work.

While they look through their phones, I continue searching around the floor. As I'm looking, an emergency weather alert goes off on all of our phones. Although, my heart race increased just a tiny bit, this time, I didn't startle as bad as I did when we got the last notification.

SPECIAL WEATHER STATEMENT
HAZARD...
*Funnel clouds, wind gusts of 55-60 mph
IMPACT... funnel clouds occasionally touch down and produce tornadoes or waterspouts. Gusty winds could knock down tree limbs and blow around unsecured objects.
*Rainfall between 6-8 inches.
*Expect flooding near streams, creaks, rivers and low drainage areas

I swipe the notification away. We should expect more of these weather alerts to go off throughout the night. Each time they appear; I can't allow myself to get startled so easily or I might actually have a real heart attack...

But never mind that. I spoke too soon about remaining calm because while I'm searching the floor, I hear Eric gasp and of course, my heart rate increases again.

"What the hell?" I irritably sigh.

"Danny had the ring on in this picture of us. We were standing by those stairs." He points to the stairs a few feet away. "The time stamp says 1:07 a.m.—"

"—But in the last picture on my phone, he's not wearing the ring and that was at two o'clock in the morning. We were in the visitor area near the front entrance because look, the front door and windows are in the background of the picture," Lucas concludes, adding onto Eric's assessment. "So then, he must've lost it over there somewhere. We were just over there."

I guess I should give these guys more credit when it comes to sensible thinking.

We leave through the door that Lucas led us through to enter this large area, and head back to the lobby with the visitor area near the front entrance.

It only takes us a few minutes of searching near the windows when I find the gold ring on the floor. "This is it!"

"Great. But we still don't know where they are," Lucas sighs.

Suddenly, our phones all blare with two more emergency alerts. This time, Lucas and Eric flinch with me.

FLOOD ADVISORY

Flood advisory in effect until tomorrow afternoon.

*WHAT.... Urban and small stream flooding, creaks, rivers, caused by excessive rainfall

*IMPACTS... ponding of water is occurring or is imminent

Be aware of your surroundings and do not drive on flooded roads.

TROPICAL STORM NOW IN EFFECT.

HAZARD... *Wind gusts up to 55-60 mph*

IMPACT... Gusty winds could knock down tree limbs and blow unsecured objects.

*Expect flooding near streams, creaks, rivers, and low drainage areas.

*Expect 6-8 inches of rain.

Tropical storms are not normally intimidating to me as I have dealt with plenty of them during my entire life of living here in Florida, but this night is freaking me out altogether. The sound of rain echoes the lobby as it slams hastily against the windows. I walk over to peer through the glass.

But when I approach the window, the storm is not what shocks me when I see what's outside...

Or rather, what I don't see.

9

E R I C

SUNDAY – 10:30 p.m.

"Is this a damn joke?!"

My baby is gone! I can't get the front door open in this shitty building because of the damn padlock on the outside. Since the door ain't allowing me out of here, I'll leave through a damn window. I unlock and lift it up effortlessly and get ready to leap through until Maddie grabs me by my shirt.

"Eric, calm down." She gives me that annoying look of disapproval; She looks just like our mother when she does this.

"No! My baby is gone! She's brand fucking new. I've only had her for a couple months. There's no way someone stole her already!" *This is ridiculous. Who would have taken my car? And why?*

It's downpouring outside but the rain ain't stopping me from going out there. Maybe I'll catch the thief driving away with her.

"Told you guys that someone else could be out here," I hear Maddie mumble just as I climb out of the window and into the storm.

I run through the front yard which is now filled with mud and water that reaches up to my ankles, lightning illuminating the sky.

I crouch down to get through the hole in the fence and run over to where my car should still be parked.

I'm too late. Whoever took her is long gone already.

Danny's truck is still parked on the side of the building outside of the fence. His windows aren't smashed or anything so I guess my beautiful brand-new car was the thief's prime target.

There ain't nobody out here right now. I don't see a tow-away sign anywhere either. Although, I wouldn't expect there to be a tow-away sign because this place is not in business and besides, who the hell would call to get my car towed?

If there were a tow-away sign, someone would have had to be around to call the number and get it towed. And nobody is out here. Regardless of what my paranoid sister thinks.

"Get back over here!" I hear the distant sound of Maddie's voice yelling at me. I turn around to see her sticking her head out of the window. "Get back in here!" She keeps yelling, just as lightning strikes nearby. "Eric! Now!"

I crouch down and crawl back through the hole in the fence, then run across the dirt filled partially flooded yard. Mud splashes around my ankles and water soaks my sneakers.

Back in the prison, I am soaking wet. Great. Just great. Now I have to spend the night in wet clothes until we get out of here.

"I can't believe someone stole her," Muttering, I take my hoodie off to hang it over a chair to dry.

"Maybe your car got towed. You did park it right out on the main street. Anyone driving by could have seen it," Maddie says. "A tow company probably came by and picked it up."

"If I don't find it at an impound lot, then I'm reporting it stolen," I mumble as I begin searching my phone for the number to the local impound lot.

"In that case, then report our friends missing too!" Maddie shrieks. "I've had enough of this night. I want to go home."

While googling for the number to the nearest impound lot, Madison struggles to pull the window back down.

"I got it." Lucas steps in front of her, implying she does not have enough strength but it looks like his strength is no match for the window either.

"What the hell, man?" He grunts. "Eric, come help me close this."

"Leave the damn thing open." I'm too preoccupied to care about a window right now. I need to figure out where my baby is.

"The window's stuck." I hear Lucas complain. "It won't close now. Rains getting in here."

While I wait for someone to answer my call, I go to pull the window down for my weak friend but he's right. The window won't close for me either.

"It's getting cold in here!" Maddie complains.

"*You're cold?* I'm the one that's soak and wet."

"You're also the one who willingly ran outside in a tropical storm," she smirks.

Nobody answers the phone when I call the impound lot. Instead, a machine tells me to input my license plate number which I don't have memorized. I do have many photos of my car though, so I find the license plate number that way.

"Guys, check your battery again. Let's not let all of our phones die while we're here

since we don't know how long we're going to
be here now. My phones at sixty-five,"
Madison says.

"Mine's at forty-seven," Lucas says.

"Eric?" Maddie eyes me.

"What? I told you what I'm doing."

"Never mind," Maddie sighs. "Lucas,
turn your flashlight off for now to save
battery. We don't all need to use our
flashlights at the same time."

"How long do you think we'll be stuck
in here?" Lucas scrunches his forehead,
concern in his expression.

"Well, without a car, it seems like we're
going to be in here longer than we planned to
be. Unless you expect us to walk home in this
storm."

"Aha! I found it. An idiot towed my
baby to a lot only three miles away," I
exclaim.

She isn't stolen after all! Oh, thank
God. I'll pay whatever fine I owe to get her
back. As long as I can get her back unharmed.
Now I need to call an Uber to pick me up
from here to go get her.

"Why wouldn't Danny's truck get
towed with yours then, too?" Lucas thinks
aloud.

"Probably because his truck wasn't
parked out in the open like Eric's was,"
Maddie retorts. "You can't even see Danny's
truck from the street. Eric parked his car right

in front of this place. Anyone driving by saw it. I bet a tow company drove by and took it."

"Thanks, Maddie." I don't need my misjudgment rubbed in my face right now. She's right. I probably should have parked my car near Danny's truck, away from the main road, but in my defense, I didn't even see his truck right away until we got out of my car. And obviously, I didn't think anyone would be out here or even care to call a tow on me.

While I request an Uber on the app, multiple emergency weather alerts simultaneously echo the room from all of our phones.

FLASH FLOOD WARNING
*WHAT... Small streams, rivers, and canals capable of flooding.
*HAZARD... Flash flooding caused by thunderstorms.
*WHERE... Everglades city, FL
PRECAUTION/PREPAREDNESS
ACTIONS....
Be aware of your surroundings and do not drive in flooded roads.

TROPICAL STORM IN EFFECT
*Winds up to 60 – 65 mph.
*Expect 6-8 inches rainfall

TORNADO WATCH

***Recreational vehicles, trailers, mobile homes, are unsafe.**
Seek shelter in a safe building

"At least we have some shelter if a tornado touches down," Lucas nervously scratches the back of his head.

"I wouldn't call this building shelter," Maddie sighs.

"We'll be fine in here. It's only a tornado watch, not a warning. That means a tornado hasn't actually touched down yet," I try to reassure her.

"Exactly. Not *yet*."

1 0

MADISON

SUNDAY 10:50 p.m.

Unless we are in a category three or higher hurricane, Floridians still go about their business when a storm hits. But apparently Ubers in this town are an exception to that fact because no one has notified Eric that they are outside yet.

The rain pelts against my face as I approach the window.

"Oh... shit. That was fast..." The front yard of the prison and the road is completely flooded. Way more flooded than it was only twenty minutes ago when Eric went out there.

The weather notifications weren't lying when they said to expect six to eight inches of rain. I can see Danny's truck from here. The water has risen up to the center of his tires already.

Eric is not getting to the impound lot in this storm. No Uber is going to drive down this street in the flood. Even if we found Danny's keys around here, his pickup truck wouldn't even be able to get through the flood without stalling or getting stuck. Maybe a lifted truck would get through (more lifted than Danny's), but we don't know anyone with a lifted truck to call to come get us.

Come to think of it, even if an Uber or anyone could pick us up if the roads weren't flooded, we more than likely wouldn't even be able to pick up Eric's car at the impound lot. He said it's only three miles down the road, so the impound lot could be flooded out too and it's already past ten o'clock. I bet nobody is there to release the car until business hours.

I refrain from telling Eric that though. He will probably just argue that I'm wrong when I know I am right.

"Where are you going?" Eric asks me when I start walking toward the hallway that we entered the lobby from.

"Away from the window," I say with a shiver.

My weather app tells me it is eighty degrees outside but the open window is bringing in a breeze from the wind and making the room chilly. It's becoming uncomfortable for my skinny body. My light blue hoodie is breaking the chill from hitting my upper body. However, my short jean shorts give me no form of warmth and goosebumps are appearing all over my legs.

"I just tried calling another Uber. Nobody wants to brave a little rain," Eric scoffs.

"That's more than a little rain out there." I shake my head.

Anger implodes all over my big brother's face; his tan skin tone turns a light shade of red. He loves his brand-new car. The thought of it suddenly being taken away from him probably really freaks him out. Probably more so than the fact that we're trapped in this building right now.

We're not in what the weather statement entitles as an unsafe vehicle or structure, but a nearly half-burned down building that probably isn't safe to stand in on a nice day is not where I want to be when it comes to riding out this storm.

"Fuck this." Suddenly, Eric grabs his hoodie from the chair, then begins to climb through the window again but I run over to stop him. "What are you doing?"

"I'm going to walk to the impound lot to get my car."

"No, you won't!" I yell, pulling him back into the building. He reluctantly allows me to pull him back, even though he has enough strength to overpower me if he wanted to. "Just wait out the storm. The radar says we're going to have a break in the rain soon."

My weather app tells me the rain will stop in about thirty-five minutes. The streets will still be flooded but the lightning should lessen by then. At least, I won't have to worry about him getting struck by lightning when he goes out there.

"No, I'm going now. You can stay here with Lucas. I'll go on my own and then you two can leave when the storm lets up. I'll wait for you in my car down the road wherever it's not flooded once I pick it up. You're not gonna walk three miles in this storm, Maddie."

My overly protective big brother has always been just that— too overly protective enough that there is no sense in arguing with him. Against my wishes and before I can tell him that he probably can't even pick his car up at this time of night, my brother climbs through the open window. Water splashes against his shins as he runs through the front yard—which is now basically a small lake.

Since the hole in the fence that we originally crawled through is covered from the floodwater, he climbs the fence instead. At first, I don't understand why he took his hoodie with him until I see him place it over the barb wire. He uses it as a barrier to crawl over the wire without getting cut.

He lands on the other side, leaving his hoodie over the fence. Water reaches up to just below his knees once he stands up on the other side of the fence where his car was once parked.

The farther he goes down the road, the higher the water rises against his body.

"Ugh, this night is causing me anxiety." I turn around to sit on one of the chairs in the lobby when suddenly Lucas gasps. "Oh, shit! That's not good…"

I turn back around to shift my eyesight toward the window and see Eric suddenly leap on top of the hood of Danny's truck.

"Something's wrong…" Lucas sticks his body out of the window to see better. "Oh, n—no, no! That's not good…"

Oh shit…

Brown murky water quickly rises over the street and causes small waves in the distance, splashing up to the door handles on Danny's truck.

"I think it's a… it's a flash flood," I realize.

The emergency alert warned us of a potential flash flood advisory of creaks, lakes, and swamps. We are literally in a building that is surrounded by a large lake. Our entire town is in the Everglades and borders the ocean. This has to be a flash flood.

In all of my twenty-nine years of living here, I've only seen a flash flood happen twice and both times were during a hurricane. Not a tropical storm. And the flood wasn't major but it was just enough to cause some damage to homes and a lot of vehicles.

"What the hell is he doing?" I gasp when suddenly, Eric leaps off the truck and begins swimming... or not really swimming, but more so, just letting the flood take him back down toward the prison.

"Oh my God... oh my...God!" I shudder. My voice has become panic-stricken. Tears involuntarily fall down my cheeks. My brother is literally being swept away by a flood and all I can do is helplessly watch it happen.

"Grab the fence!" Lucas yells, although it must be impossible for Eric to hear him through the heavy rain, howling wind, thunder and the raging floodwater coming our way.

But either Eric already had it in mind to grab the fence or he heard Lucas tell him because suddenly, Eric smacks his body against the fence when he grabs onto it and begins climbing over.

"Hurry!" Lucas and I both shout in unison as we watch the flood rise higher and flow into the open window we're yelling out of. Water splashes on the floor and over our shoes.

Eric did not grab the part of the fence where he left his hoodie over the barbwire, so he is forced to climb over the wire without the barrier this time. He jumps off the fence and lands in the front yard before wading through the floodwater to climb back through the window of the prison.

After he gets through, soaked and heavily breathing, we all grab onto the window and push it down together. Thankfully, the combined force of our strength, and maybe our adrenaline too, allows the window to shut completely.

"We should've tried that earlier," I mumble.

Gasping for breath, Eric leans onto his knees. That's when I notice blood dripping down his legs and hands. A piece of his shorts are torn off.

"Oh my God! You're bleeding! The barbwire cut you!"

"No shit," he mutters. "I didn't even think twice about it. I had no other choice or else I would have gotten stuck out there. I'm fine. It's just a little blood. We should get to the second floor just in case the flood makes it in through the burned side of the building and knocks down the plywood. I don't think the water will get in here that quickly, but when it does, we shouldn't be down here."

At this point, I am almost positive Danny and Oliver are not here. And if they are, then they are in far more danger than we can handle. We can't even call the police because at this point, nobody is going to come save us. They physically can't come out here in this weather. We're stuck here until this storm passes.

11

MADISON

SUNDAY - 11:15 p.m.

"Okay, now I'm really starting to get worried about Danny and Oliver," Lucas says while pacing back and forth on the second floor above the stairs.

"Now you're getting worried?" I lean back against the top step when I sit down on the step below it.

Up here, the second floor is formed in a circle. It's just as dark on this floor as it is on the first floor. Several inmate cells—probably at least fifty or more, another medical room (this one with the sign *OPERATING AREA*), and a security room, which is where we are sitting in front of) take up the entire floor.

Eric lost his phone in the flood, so we are only left with mine and Lucas's phones to use for flashlights. Since Lucas's phone has less battery than mine, he's keeping it off until we need another light. I am the only light source up here and it's not giving us much to see.

"At least we're safe here for now," Eric says. "The water definitely won't reach this high if the flood does make it into the building."

"That's if the building remains standing," I mutter. "And we're not safe up here if a tornado hits."

"We're still only in a tornado watch. Not a warning. Don't worry about it," Eric shrugs.

"DANNY! OLIVER!" Lucas yells, slightly startling me.

"If they're here, then they would've made themselves known already," Eric says exactly what I was just thinking.

Shocker because he is the more positive sibling out of us. I guess getting stuck out in a flood really takes the optimism out of a person.

"And that's probably because they can't make themselves known," I mumble, adding onto the pessimism. I don't want to be negative, but I am thinking rationally. If our friends are here, then they must not be in a good physical state to answer us.

"Stop saying shit like that," Lucas scoffs, his voice raised. I stare at him in disbelief. Lucas has never yelled at me like that before.

"Relax, man." Eric rests his hand on Lucas's shoulder, gently shaking him.

"This is not a relaxing situation." Lucas stomps ahead of us. Despite our agreement to stay off his phone to save battery, he turns on his flashlight and starts looking in each of the cells as he trudges down the hall. "Danny! Oliver!"

While Lucas looks in the cells ahead of us, I get up from the stairs and follow Eric inside the medical room.

We first see a broken overhead light over a metal operating table in the middle of the room. Cabinets are left open, revealing medical forms and inmate files along with biohazard jars inside. Vials of very old blood and bags of IVs are scattered all over the floor. I carefully step around everything. More inmate files with their mugshots and medical information are dispersed on the counter of the surgical area. Oliver and Danny are obviously not in here and I've seen all I needed to see.

Eric and I are about to leave when something clatters on the ground. At first, I think the sound came from in the room with us until I realize Eric didn't bump into anything. Neither did I.

It had to be Lucas.

We walk out of the room to find Lucas coming out of an inmate cell a couple of feet down the hall.

"What happened?" Eric asks him.

"I don't know. I thought y'all made that noise," Lucas answers.

"Wasn't us either." Eric exchanges a worried glance to me and takes my phone out of my hand to shine the light down the hallway behind us.

"It sounded close," I whisper.

"Oliv—"

"Shh!" I slap Lucas's arm.

"What the hell, Maddie?"

"What if that's not Oliver and Danny?" I hastily whisper. "Be quiet!"

Eric starts to take a step toward where the noise sounded like it came from, but I grab him by the back of his shirt.

"Who else would it be?" he whispers.

I give him an obvious look, but both Lucas and Eric do not seem to catch on because they are looking at me like I've grown an extra head.

"It could literally be anyone. You think we're the first ones to break in here? That side door we got in here through was more than likely open for a reason. Anyone else could be lurking around here."

"It's probably just teenagers," Lucas says.

"I doubt that. We would have heard teenagers by now. Teenagers are normally loud and they don't know how to stay quiet," I argue.

"Or the noise came from Danny and Oliver!" Lucas argues back.

"But then why haven't they answered us when we were calling them, if it is them?" Eric murmurs.

"Because it's probably not them, guys!" I sigh as I look at Eric. Although, I know the answer to my question, I ask anyway. "You left your gun in the car, didn't you?"

He nods. "I can't carry it on me in these shorts. They'll fall off my waist if I do. And I would have lost my gun in the flood if I brought it with me anyway. Shit, I'm glad I didn't bring it."

"Great. Just great," I mutter.

"Relax. I'm not shooting anyone anyway, Maddie," Eric shakes his head. "If it's not them, then it's probably an animal or something."

"Well, I'm finding out what that noise was." Lucas begins walking down the hall.

Eric grabs my arm, forcing me to reluctantly follow them. When we are a few feet down the hall, I realize I'm gripping onto Eric's arm extra tightly. I don't know when I tightened my grip like this, but I have no plans on letting go. It's not because he has my phone and I need to follow him closely or I'll get left behind in the dark. I am gripping onto him because everything in my body is raising an alarm. Fight or flight is kicking in and I think we should choose flight.

No... actually, *I know* we should choose flight. But I can't choose flight alone, and it's physically impossible to choose flight with the flood and storm outside, so I am forced to follow my brother and Lucas who are both foolishly following fight.

A clattering noise suddenly echoes the hallway again. This time louder and closer. My heart sinks as Lucas points his phone's flashlight across the hall toward the other end of the floor where there are more inmate cells.

While all of the cell doors remain closed, at the end of the hallway just before the floor curves back around, there is one door that is slightly propped open by a stack of books. We never noticed the open door before until we rounded the corner.

Lucas quickens his steps, taking the lead toward the open door. Eric follows him as I continue clinging on his arm.

As we reach only a few feet near the door, I attempt to pull Eric back. "Guys, we should turn—"

But it's too late to convince them to turn around when a can of tear gas rolls out onto the hallway from inside of the cell and lands only a few feet in front of us.

12

MADISON

SUNDAY - 11:45 p.m.

My face crashes against Eric's arm when I bump into him as he abruptly stops walking at the sight of the tear gas canister. At first, I brace myself for the impact from tear gas to spray until I realize nothing is spraying at us. The can must be empty.

The door that is propped up by books creaks loudly as it abruptly opens wider.

In an orange inmate uniform, heavy black boots on his feet, and very disheveled looking, a tall man—taller than my six-foot two brother, shines a large flashlight right at us.

His flashlight washes out the light from mine and Lucas's cell phones.

The man angrily shouts as he takes a step toward us. "What the hell do you want?"

"Aye, man! We're not here to cause any harm," Lucas quickly answers. He puts his hands up in a gesture to show we're unarmed.

Not such a smart move. We have no idea what this stranger has on him besides that flashlight. He could have a gun. A weapon of some kind. More tear gas that might actually work. We can't even see the guys face that well because of the flashlight in our own faces.

"Me neither," the man grudgingly responds. "What are you doing here?"

"What are *you* doing here?" Lucas retorts.

"I live here!" The man grunts. Irritation builds in his voice as he takes a step closer toward us.

"Were you an inmate here?" Lucas eyes him without backing away.

"Just needed a place to stay," the guy says. "Now, tell me what the hell are you all doing here?"

I do not like that this guy can see us so clearly in the light and we can barely see him. He has more of an advantage on us and since Lucas volunteered that we're unarmed, nothing about this confrontation is good. I knew we weren't alone in here. I could feel it from the moment we got out of Eric's car.

"We're looking for our friends," Eric responds.

"Have you seen these guys?" Lucas asks and my eyes nearly bulge out of my head when he walks right up to the man to show him a picture of Danny and Oliver.

What another stupid move— getting close to a man dressed in a stolen inmate uniform who is clearly angry that we're here. Oh, and we still have no idea what weapon he has on him, if he has one at all. Whether this guy is actually an ex-inmate, homeless or both, his demeanor is not friendly toward us. He obviously does not want us here.

Wait... I wonder if this guy is one of the few inmates who escaped during the fire.

The majority of the inmates that survived the fire here got out safely and were transferred to another prison. Only a few of them (from what I remember hearing in the news) actually escaped. Whether they were ever caught, I have no idea.

But there's no way, this guy could be one of those who escaped... Why would he come back to a place he originally escaped from?

Then again, who would come looking for him here after all these years? Especially since this place is abandoned. Maybe he is one of the escapees after all.

Now I have the urge to look up the inmate escapee story. I'll wait to pull out my phone until we get away from him.

"Never seen em'." The guy shakes his head. He barely even glances at the picture on Lucas's phone.

"Alright, well we'll just let you be. Sorry to disturb you," Eric says, then nudges Lucas. "Come on, man. Let's go."

The disheveled man says nothing and remains standing in the hallway with his arms crossed.

I quickly turn around to head back down the hallway while still keeping my grip tightly around my brother's arm. As we walk away, I can feel the man's eyes pierce through me. I can't help it. For some reason, I need to glance over my shoulder.

The creep points his flashlight on his face. He smiles and gives me a wink.

I quickly turn back around without taking a second glance.

We round the corner, and head down the stairs to the other security room on the first floor. A deafening crash of thunder rattles the building. Rain pounds against the building and the wind howls outside.

Cringing, I grab a dirty rolling office chair in front of the broken computers and sit on the edge of the seat. If I stand around down here, my anxiety will only heighten.

"Y'all think that dude was a prisoner here before?" asks Lucas which reminds me to look up the prisoner escapee story.

"Nah, I think he's just homeless." Eric spins around in his chair while looking up at all the broken TV's that are mounted on the wall above the computers. "He's probably just living here and that cell he walked out of was his makeshift house. If you think about it, this place is a pretty good spot to stay low key in for a homeless person. No security here. He's got a roof over his head."

I keep my thought about the man possibly being one of the inmates that escaped after the fire to myself. Eric will just tell me that I am overthinking and being dramatic. He could be right but he could also be very wrong.

So far, I find nothing to back up my thought process. None of the mugshots of the escapees resemble the man we just saw. Then again, I didn't even see his face clearly (only for a moment before I turned away) and it's been seven years since the fire. He could be any one of these guys, but with drastic changes now. I would have no idea.

Thunder rumbles outside and jolts the prison. The storm is only intensifying. The weather channel said the hurricane is supposed to hit the east coast instead of where we are which is on the Gulf coast. But as the night goes on, it feels like it's turning into a category one hurricane instead.

I check my phones radar to see if anything has changed with the path of the hurricane.

Nope. No change. The weather app says the hurricane is predicted to still hit the east coast only. Our town is only supposed to get the outer bands of the storm which will be the "dirty" side of the hurricane. That means we are likely to actually see a tornado hit or even a few that will touch down, along with a lot of strong wind and rain which we are already getting.

My anxiety is rising every minute we are stuck here. Especially now after having the run in with that possible escaped inmate. I really wish I was home drinking a bottle of wine and watching Netflix instead. Although, I would still be a nervous wreck if I knew Eric and Lucas went here alone to search for Danny and Oliver. Which speaking of, I'm getting more worried about them as the night goes on too.

"I wish we got to see inside of the cell the guy came out of," I say.

Lucas gives me a strange look. "Why would you want to see in his cell? There's probably a bunch of shit in it. I could smell it when I got closer to him."

"Why do you think, idiot?" I know I am being mean, but I have to call out his stupidity. I am not sure if Lucas is just naturally clueless or if it's an act sometimes.

Or if he is just as positive as Eric and doesn't show it like Eric does. Lucas is my friend, but he really gets on my nerves. Especially tonight. "What if Oliver and Danny were in his cell tied up or something?"

"You need to stop watching so many thriller movies and crime documentaries," Lucas scoffs, clearly enraged that I called him out on his stupidity.

"I don't even watch that many! I'm using common sense. Just because it's more common for women to get raped and kidnapped, doesn't mean that can't happen to men too! I know that's out of the norm to hear, but this whole night is out of the norm! I'm not saying I hope that happened to either of them... *but it is a possibility.* We have to think rationally. Danny's truck is outside and we found his ring, so where else could they be? We need to get inside that guy's cell. I bet they're in there."

"Yeah, but Oliver and Danny are big guys. They can handle themselves," Lucas says.

"Nobody can handle or defend themself if they're taken by surprise. Or if the other person has a weapon and they don't which we know they didn't. Danny and Oliver don't carry guns." Sighing out of frustration, I unlock my phone, ready to dial 9-1-1. "I don't care if we get arrested or get fined or whatever consequence happens for being here. I don't care if the police can't come right away because of the flood. I'm still calling to let them know what's going—"

"No, you're not!" Lucas urgently shouts. Again, raising his voice at me for a second time tonight.

"Shh! We can't let that weirdo hear us!" I hastily whisper. "We shouldn't let him know where we are."

"That guy can't hear us from down here. The storm is too loud outside. Besides, we're on a completely different floor than he is. You need to relax, Maddie." Lucas begins pacing.

"Are you kidding me right now?" I grit my teeth in disbelief.

First it was Eric telling me to relax, now it's Lucas. Do they want me to punch them? Relax, right now? Relax, when our friends are missing, we're in a tornado watch, a flash flood has us trapped in an unsafe building and we're literally stuck here with a random guy whose probably an escaped inmate, dangerous, and clearly does not like that we're here.

But sure, I'll relax.

"What's going on with you, man?" Eric asks Lucas.

Lucas exhales. "I didn't want to say anything after Danny's dad died in the way he did. But I might as well tell y'all now. I spent the night in the drunk tank a few nights before we took Danny to the bar and ended up here. I can't have another charge on my record or it'll look bad on me as a father. If you call the cops and we get arrested or even a fine for being here, my ex-wife could use it against me and file for full custody."

"Oh, so that's why you're being snippy with me," I scoff.

"You got put in the drunk tank? Don't tell me you drove drunk." Eric shakes his head in disappointment because of how Danny's dad died.

Inadvertently, the alcoholic didn't die because he was drunk. He died because of another drunk slamming into him instead. And to make matters worse, he didn't even pass away instantly. He suffered for hours after in the ICU until his spleen ruptured.

"Yeah. I fucked up. I drove drunk and got pulled over. Which I'm glad I did get pulled over because I could have seriously killed someone... or myself. That's why I didn't tell y'all yet especially so soon after Danny's dad died. Now I have a DUI on my record, which is better than you know, being dead or killing someone else. Just don't tell Danny. He'll fucking kill me if he knew what I did."

"That's if he's not dead yet," I mumble and this time, Eric slaps my arm.

"Quit it." He scolds me.

"It's pretty ironic how Danny always worried about alcohol killing his dad when a drunk ended up killing the guy instead," I say the words out loud that none of us has spoken yet. Not even Danny.

"No need to state the obvious, Maddie," Lucas snaps.

Okay, he's right. I should've kept that thought to myself. I didn't mean to pour salt in his wound but hey, that's just my personality.

"I wouldn't have come here the other night if I didn't get so drunk with y'all. I only went out drinking because it was your idea, man." He looks at Eric. "I wasn't worried about driving obviously, since we called the Uber but I didn't expect to come here. Not then and not now. I wasn't gonna leave you guys to come look for Danny and Oliver alone tonight though."

"Nah, don't put all the blame on me. It wasn't my idea to go to the bar or come here after. You can thank Oliver for that."

"Whatever. I'll give him shit about it when we find him."

I hold back what I really want to say as Eric shoots me one of our telepathic sibling looks. *Keep your mouth shut. Don't add on to the disappointment in what Lucas just admitted.*

I get it, big bro.

Being pessimistic in this situation does not help anyone. Although, I wouldn't call myself pessimistic. It's not pessimism if I am thinking realistically. We are in a seriously dangerous situation and I had a bad feeling about this night from the moment I got out of the car. It's killing me not to say 'I told you so'.

Lucas sighs. "I don't remember being here at all the other night. If it weren't for the pictures and videos on our phones, I wouldn't think the other night even happened, honestly. I was hammered."

"Yeah. I get it," Eric agrees.

Pictures and videos. I face palm my forehead. Hanging around these guys really has caused my own common sense to dwindle. We figured out how to find Danny's ring by looking back through our phones, so then we need to do the same thing to actually find Oliver and Danny. I start to scroll on my phone again to look at my own gallery.

"Lucas, look at your pictures and videos again from the other night. Maybe we'll notice something that will tell us where Danny and Oliver might be tonight. We can't really remember anything, so maybe a photo or video will give us something new— somewhere new to look around here. We haven't explored every single room and area yet."

While Lucas looks through his phone again, I re-watch a couple of videos on my own phone. Most of the videos are downstairs around the area of where I wrote my name on the wall. I scroll through the pictures that I took of Oliver when we were alone, which is on the second floor near where the disheveled guy's cell is.

Nothing seems out of the ordinary in our photos until I spot something in the background behind Oliver and I. We're standing near the security room upstairs.

"Oh my God..." Gasping, I nearly drop my phone. I can finally pinpoint what that eerie discomforting feeling that has been hovering over me is.

Silently with my teeth clenched, I zoom into the background of the photo and turn my phone screen to face the guys. I'm speechless.

"Oh, what the hell?" Eric snatches the phone out of my hand to get a better view, gasping when he sees the background too.

In the photo, the same disheveled man in the inmate uniform who we just faced upstairs, stands at the doorway of a nearby cell behind us. He holds an axe over his shoulder as he stares right into mine and Oliver's back.

13

ERIC

MONDAY – 12:00 a.m.

"H—holy shit!" Maddie shudders. "How the hell didn't I notice that guy behind us when we took this picture?"

I have heard my sister panic before but never like she's panicking right now. Terror is plastered all over her face as she stares at the photo on her phone.

"Alright. I guess Maddie was right. We *do* need to see what's in that dude's cell." Lucas runs his hands through his hair as he begins pacing around the security room.

"You mean, we need to see *who's in there? Not what,*" Maddie retorts.

"Shut up! Both of you!" I need to think and Madison's cynical attitude and Lucas's combative personality is not helping me focus right now.

"Okay, there are two of us and one of him," I say as Lucas passes by me.

"Uhm, you mean three of us?" Maddie interjects.

"Hell no! You're not going near that guy again. You're staying right here." I stand up to pace alongside Lucas.

Maddie scoffs a sarcastic laugh. "So, you guys just plan to leave me alone here while you go snooping around an axe murderer's cell?"

She makes a good point but I prefer that she does not get close to that guy if she doesn't need to. The three of us pass each other within every step in this small dark security room as we all pace together. Something about walking back and forth gives us false hope that moving around is keeping us calm.

A series of lightning strikes and thunder booms outside, rattling the building... and our nerves.

So much for trying to stay calm.

"Well, we don't know that he's an actual murderer. He could have just been holding the axe." As soon as the words leave my mouth, Lucas and Maddie stop pacing and stare at me.

"Are you really *that* optimistic?" Maddie slaps my arm. "He had an axe over his shoulder. He wasn't just holding it for no reason. He's a murderer."

"He could have just been defending his home from us," I say. I am not trying to defend the man. I am just trying to look at a safer explanation; a reason that won't allow me to believe we're in actual danger. "If he wanted to kill us, then he would have tried the other night. I don't think he has intent to harm us. He had that opportunity the first night we were here."

"I'm not so sure about that," Maddie disagrees. "We were all drunk the other night. Drunk people tend to be more annoying to sober people, and harder to probably kill."

"Like you would know," Lucas mutters.

"It's called common sense."

"Enough, both of you."

They both need to stop arguing because I can't think straight.

"We can't just stay down here all night without making sure Danny and Oliver aren't in there," I decide. "Lucas will go back to the cell with me. Maddie, you keep a look out from down here. We'll be gone for only a few minutes."

"You guys can't go back to his cell while he's there. You think he's going to invite you right in? You need to wait for him to leave," she hastily whispers, even though, there is no way that guy can hear us down here with the storm roaring outside of the building.

She makes a good point though. We do have to wait for the guy to leave. In that case, Maddie shouldn't be alone when that happens. She has to come with us when we go back.

"We need a weapon before we go back upstairs though," I decide. "Just in case he comes back to the cell when we're in there. We don't know if that guy has a weapon on him."

"Uh, we know he has a damn axe," Maddie mumbles as she reluctantly shines her phone's flashlight inside another cabinet.

"Besides the axe," I say.

Maddie may be annoyingly pessimistic but she makes a good point. Regardless of whether I'm right, the guy upstairs either uses the axe to defend his home, or if Maddie's right and he's a killer, we need something to combat him.

"Tear gas!" Lucas suddenly says with a breath of excitement. "He had tear gas! I know the can didn't go off, but there's got to be more of those canisters somewhere around here."

"But if we find any, then they're probably empty or too old to work anymore," Maddie says. "That's probably why nothing sprayed out of the can that the psycho rolled out at us. I bet he didn't even know the can was empty. I bet he rolled it out into the hallway in hopes that it would spray us. He was probably just as shocked as we were when nothing came out of it."

Lucas pulls out a bunch of inmate files from the drawers and cabinets in the security desk, then tosses the files on the ground. "Well, unless we plan to throw papers at him, there's nothing in here that will defend us. Let's go check the other security room upstairs. I remember seeing lockers in that one."

He's right. This first-floor security room must've been more for paperwork and surveillance of the second floor where the inmate cells are, hence the TV's. The security room that we passed by upstairs is bigger and has a couple of lockers. I would assume there is protective gear for the police in them.

"There isn't even a flashlight down here," Maddie sighs as she closes a drawer.

"Hopefully, we'll find one upstairs then," says Lucas before leaving the room. He heads toward the stairs, leaving us no other choice but to follow him.

In the security room on the second floor, we all start searching the lockers. I cannot find anything useful but Lucas does. At least, he thinks he does.

"This should work," he says when pulling out a body armor vest.

It looks heavy as he struggles to pull it over his head and places it on his chest over his shirt. I am surprised he so willingly put that dirty thing on his body. Lucas isn't necessarily the type of guy to be the first to jump in a puddle of mud to push a truck out or to get on his hands and knees to change a tire.

"I don't think that body armor will help you," Maddie mutters. "Pretty sure that won't stop an axe."

"If it stops bullets, it sure as hell will stop an Axe," Lucas contends.

"If you say so," she mutters.

I'm with my sister on this one. Body armor definitely will not stop an axe but I'll let Lucas believe what he wants to believe right now. No sense in arguing.

Maddie kicks a pile of inmate uniforms and shoes on the ground in front of a locker so she can open it.

"Ah! That's what I'm talking about!" Lucas says, excitedly when we see a pile of tear gas and mace canisters, along with two large flashlights in the locker.

One flashlight is very dim when it turns on while the other one is completely dead. There aren't any batteries laying around either, not that they would probably work after all these years. This dim flashlight is not casting nearly as much light as the flashlight that the guy was holding did, but this will still do. At least, we have another light option besides Lucas and Maddie's phones.

Although Maddie is probably right about the canisters being empty, it still won't hurt to check them anyway. Lucas and I begin picking the canisters up and shaking them to see if they are full or not.

"Don't spray any!" Maddie gasps when she sees Lucas's finger on the nozzle of a can.

"Relax, I wasn't going to spray it. This one is empty anyway," he says. "All of these are empty."

"Empty here too." I move on to check another locker. When I open the door, more canisters fall out onto the floor and over my shoes. Most of them feel empty when I pick them up, except for two.

"Yes! I think these two are full!" I keep one and hand the other to Lucas. Maddie attempts to grab the one out of my hand but I yank it away. "You can hold the flashlight we found."

"A flashlight isn't going to defend me. You guys realize those cans might not even spray if you need them because they're like, several years old, right? I wouldn't rely on those."

"You've already said that," I tell her. "This is all we got though so we just have to hope for the best." I know she's right about the tear gas cans. It's unlikely they'll still work if we have to use them, but it is worth a shot in taking them with us anyway, because you never know. If we need them, we might get lucky.

"Fine. Do what you want." She throws her hands up. "But I'm going to get my own weapon."

Before I can talk her out of whatever she is about to do, she leaves the security room. For someone who is so paranoid and scared of the deranged axe wielding homeless guy, why would she go off on her own? My sister contradicts herself without even realizing it.

"Maddie!" I irritably whisper outside of the doorway to see where she went. Then I see her walk out of a cell near the medical room where she wrote her name on the wall with a police baton stick in her hand.

Smiling, she holds it over her shoulder like a bat. "I saw this in here when we walked by earlier. Don't even dare try to take this from me."

Let her have it. It's probably better that a man doesn't confront another man with a weapon at first anyway. If shit does go awry, I'll just yank the baton stick out of her hand. It's not like she will have the confidence to use the thing against the guy anyway. No offense to my sister, but she doesn't have an aggressive bone in her body. I know she's scared tonight.

And admittedly, so am I. Well, not scared... but unnerved.

14

MADISON

MONDAY – 12:20 a.m.

We are still under a tornado watch.

We're still stuck in an unsafe building with a guy carrying an axe around.

And we're still flooded out.

The only way this night will get better is when we find Danny and Oliver safe and sound.

The door to the cell of the likely axe murderer remains partially opened, propped up by a stack of books on the floor, allowing a gleam of light to shine out into the hallway from inside.

"Aye, man! You in there?" Lucas shouts as we approach the door.

Eric and I shoot him a thwarting look. *What a smart idea; Alert the man who carries an axe that we're coming back to confront him.*

When we don't hear the man respond, Lucas takes the opportunity to walk right into the cell.

What another smart idea.

Neither of us can stop Lucas from making poor choices before thinking his decisions all the way through. Oliver's lack of thinking normally overshadows Lucas which is why it is now becoming more apparent that Lucas and Oliver are basically the same person. They don't think before they react.

"Whoa! Y'all come in here!" Lucas calls out to us.

"No! Let's turn back around!" I grab Eric's arm to pull him back from stepping forward, but he yanks it away from me.

"Come on, everything will be fine," Eric foolishly tries to reassure me once again when I know in fact, nothing about tonight is fine. "You said it yourself. We need to see if Danny and Oliver are in there," he says.

I reluctantly follow him. The stench of the cell immediately makes me gag the moment I step inside. Oliver and Danny aren't in here. However, I didn't expect to see everything else that is.

Colorful battery powered Christmas lights are strung up alongside the wall. The gleam of light that shone into the hallway comes from a large flashlight (same as the dim one we found in the security room) that's placed on a night stand. A pile of orange inmate uniforms with other items that I can't make out and definitely won't touch, sit on the top bunk. Yellow stained sheets are on the bottom bunk bed— I assume that's where the psycho sleeps.

On the other side of the cell, a messy pile of books sits on the floor next to the nasty urinal. The axe that I spotted in the back of my picture leans up against the wall right next to it. The tip of the axe is dark red, almost a dark brown color.

Is that dried blood?

Shining the dim flashlight on it, I hesitantly take a step closer, as if the thing is magically going to pick itself up and slash me in half.

Yeah... That definitely looks like dried blood. Since the blood isn't dripping, it's obviously not fresh which I guess is a good sign...

But nonetheless, that is still blood.

"This man is a sick fuck," Eric scowls. He hovers over Lucas who is shining his flashlight around the bottom bunk bed.

"Let's get the hell out of here!" I turn away from the axe, but then I'm startled by my own findings when I see a cracked phone screen poking out from a pile of newspapers on the nightstand. "Whoa... wait a second..."

With my elbow, I move the newspapers away, revealing a phone with a cracked screen. Using the sleeve of my hoodie over my index finger and thumb, (which I can't wait to throw this hoodie out once we get out of here after touching all this nasty stuff) I carefully pick up the phone.

This is Oliver's. I recognize the black skulls on the case. While shoving his phone into the pocket of my hoodie, I search underneath the rest of the newspapers when a blue phone case sticks out at me. "Guys—"

Just as I pick up the second phone, which must be Danny's but I can't tell because it's turned off and I can't remember what his phone case looks like, Lucas startles me. "Whoa, man! Be cool!" he says.

At the same time, a light shines in on us, illuminating the entire cell. Swiftly, I shove the second phone in the same pocket of my hoodie before turning around and stepping behind Eric. With shaky hands, I tighten my grip around the baton stick.

Okay, maybe I should have given this to my brother instead.

The psycho points his flashlight at us. He clears his throat. "Get out of my fucking house!"

As he stands there, I come to the chilling realization that we are all cornered in this room. In order to get by him, he needs to move out of the doorway. And he could easily lock us in here from the hallway. All he has to do is shut the door and turn the lock from the outside. That is, if we don't move quick enough to stop him.

But he doesn't have a weapon on him. The axe is only about two feet to the right of me instead. He probably wouldn't lock us in here with his own weapon... right?

Then again, who knows what else he has hiding underneath his clothes?

And why doesn't he have the axe on him in the first place?

Maybe Eric *is* right. Maybe he doesn't deem us as threatening.

Well, if he didn't deem us as a threat before, he does now. Especially after finding us snooping around here and seeing Lucas with body armor on like he's ready for war, and a police baton stick in my hand.

"Get out," the guy repeats without budging from the doorway.

Lucas takes the lead and steps toward the guy with his hands up in the air. "Whoa! Sorry, man. We were just looking for our friends. We'll leave you alone."

"I told you they aren't here. Get out."

As Eric moves to follow Lucas, I realize this guy is going to figure out that I took Oliver's and Danny's phones eventually.

And it's too late to put the phones back now.

He's going to know that we know he's lying about knowing where they are. The phones in my pocket prove it. But Eric and

Lucas don't know I have Danny and Oliver's phones yet. If I tell them now, they will most likely start an altercation with this guy and I can't allow them to escalate this situation. Lucas already looks like he is ready for a fight with that bulky body armor on him.

It is either very clear to this guy that we are wary of him or he might just think Lucas is an idiot. Either way, both conclusions are right.

Although, the police baton stick is in my hand and the axe is right next to us if we do need to fight him, so maybe I should show the guys the phones before we walk out of here...

But before I can decide whether we should inflict violence or not, the man steps out of the doorway and into the hallway, lowering his flashlight out of our faces.

Lucas walks out first with his hands at his sides, palms out. I follow Eric while keeping the baton stick down at my side, avoiding eye contact with the psycho.

We quickly walk down the hall. Before turning the corner to reach the stairs, I glance over my shoulder. To my surprise, the likely axe murderer is out of sight already. His door bounces off the book stack against the doorframe, leaving a glimpse of light cascading into the hallway. I have a thought to run back and shut the door completely, in hopes that it will lock him inside of the cell, but I think better of it and continue following my brother and Lucas to the stairs.

Downstairs, the three of us reconvene in the hallway right outside of the door that leads to the main lobby where the front entrance is. The floodwater has made its way through the plywood on the burned side of the building and has risen to just above our ankles over here.

While I prefer to be behind the door in the area where the water hasn't invaded yet or upstairs with dry shoes, I rather have soggy wet socks and sneakers than remain on the same floor and in the same area with a likely deranged axe killer.

I pull the phones out of my hoodie. "Look what I found. These are Oliver and Danny's!" I gesture to the phone with the blue case. "At least, I think this phone is Danny's. I know this other one is Oliver's because of the skulls. I told you that guy knows where they are."

"Why didn't you tell us that upstairs?" Eric grabs the phones from me and attempts to turn them on.

Danny's phone turns on right away with fifteen percent battery left, but Oliver's doesn't turn on at all. I assume the psycho must've turned the phones off and Oliver's phone won't turn on because it doesn't have enough charge.

"I didn't think it was a good idea to show you in front of him. We need to find

Danny and Oliver first. It's not like the psycho will just willingly tell us what he did to them or why he has their phones. Now we know something happened to them in here. I told you something was wrong!"

"We still don't know anything yet," Eric says.

"Damnit, I got to take this thing off. It's getting too hot." Lucas wipes away the sweat on his forehead as he pulls the body armor vest over his head and sets it on the floor in the flood. "Shit, I could barely breathe with that thing on me."

I refrain from telling him how much of a dumb idea it was to wear the vest in the first place. Now that the guy saw him wearing it, along with the baton stick in my hand, we definitely came off as a threat to him. Even though we walked out of his cell willingly, the guy must know we're ready to fight him if need be. I can only assume he didn't attack us while we were cornered in his cell because we were closer to his murder weapon than he was.

I'm just glad Lucas didn't spontaneously try to set off a tear gas can on him.

Eric paces in front of the door that we just walked out of, creating a small wave of floodwater that splashes against our ankles.

"We haven't looked everywhere in this place for them yet. We still have to look around the burned side of the building," Eric says as he gestures down the hallway.

"Then let's go," I say, impatiently. "The longer we wait, the higher the water is going to get over there."

To further my point, rain slams the windows near the front entrance. The glass rattles so violently, I wonder if the windows are at risk of shattering.

"Oh... shit," Lucas widens his eyes, feeling around his jean pockets.

"What now?" I groan.

"My keys... I think I dropped my keys in the dude's cell."

"How? Why?" I groan again. "Why would you think that?"

"Because I thought I heard something drop when the dude came back and I turned around. I just realized my keys aren't in my pocket. I had them with me when we got here."

"Well, you'll just have to get new keys," I say.

"I can't! That keyring has my house key, my car key and the key to my parent's house. It's not that easy to just get new keys. I'm gonna go back to look for them."

"Okay, now you're just asking for a confrontation if you do that. I'm sorry but that is a really stupid idea. That guy does not want any of us in his little makeshift house. He made that very clear."

This isn't the time to sugarcoat the situation. We're in deep shit and our friends, are in even deeper, metaphorically and probably literally.

Suddenly, two emergency weather notifications blare from mine, Lucas and Danny's phones.

We rush to silence them immediately.

Even though we are on the other side of the door and on another floor from the psycho's cell, I don't trust that he isn't nearby. Who knows if he stayed upstairs after we left? What if he's somewhere on the burned side of the building watching us now? This building is a complete maze and navigating it in the dark isn't easy.

To the psycho though, I bet he has no problem.

After all, he was lurking around us the first night we were here. And clearly, by the photo that I spotted him in from that night, he got pretty close to me and Oliver without us even knowing. Then again, we were all extremely incoherent. Thinking logically, it's probably pretty easy to maneuver around a group of people who aren't paying attention to their surroundings, especially intoxicated, and don't realize that they are in harm's way.

TROPICAL STORM IN EFFECT
***FLOODING ADVISORY of small creaks, lakes, and small bodies of water**
***EXPECT WINDS OF 60-65 MPH**

***Rainfall 8-9 inches**

TORNADO WATCH IN EFFECT
***Mobile homes, recreational vehicles
are unsafe***

Unless the axe murderer actually attempts to kill us, then this night literally can't get any worse.

1 5

L U C A S

MONDAY – 12:45 a.m.

My shoes are submerged in this nasty bacterium filled water down here and it's making me want to gag.

Once we get out of here alive, I'm fighting my ex-wife about the day care situation. There will be no more unnecessary days of me not being with my son. I wouldn't have agreed to come back here if he was with me for the night. If he had been with me, I would be home in my bed while he peacefully sleeps in his own bed across the hall, only a few feet away from me instead. Both of us safe.

Yes, I know how selfish it sounds to think this way, but my friends would be dealing with this themselves and I would not have a fear of not living another day to see my son. Danny and Oliver are my best friends. But if I have to choose between them and my son, I should always choose my son.

I should have thought about him tonight even though he's at his mom's for the night. I should not have put myself in another dangerous situation, like I did when I drove drunk. I could've killed myself driving drunk and here I am again, at risk of dying because I'm trapped here with a probable killer... as Maddie keeps implying.

For once, I think she might be right about the dude. There could be no good reason for him to be walking around with an axe... none at all.

I'm ashamed in my choices. Here I am, risking leaving my son to live his life without a father.

Hell, screw thinking about my terrible choices. I *will* live another day to see my son. The three of us are getting out of here no matter what tonight.

Actually, all five of us are getting out of here. We came here to find Danny and Oliver and that's what we're going to do. I can't allow myself to think like Maddie does. Danny and Oliver have to be okay.

They *need* to be okay.

Thunder crashes outside and the wind rattles the building. This storm is nasty. The weather station swears this is a tropical storm, yet it feels like it's on the verge of a category one hurricane. I wouldn't be surprised if we hear the track of the storm changes and gets upgraded to a hurricane on our side of town. Which I really hope it doesn't because the sooner the storm is over, the sooner we can get out of here safely.

First, we need to find Danny and Oliver though. I was hesitant to believe something bad happened to them here but now after Maddie found their phones, and seeing the photo of the dude with the axe, it's hard not to believe that he is the reason why they're missing.

Since my phone has thirty-two percent left, Danny's is on fifteen, and Maddie's is on thirty-five, we are keeping the flashlights off on all of the phones. For now, the only light source we are using is the dim flashlight that we found in the security room until it dies. I need to save my battery in case my ex-wife calls me about my son. God forbid, there is an emergency. Not that I'd be able to do anything about it since I am literally stuck in this building, but she should still be able to contact me if she needs to.

If only she knew where I am tonight. It would just give her more fuel in a custody battle. She's never tried to take full custody of him but, in this instance, I wouldn't put it past her. Thanks to Oliver's picture of us on his profile, she wouldn't have even known I came here in the first place the other night. That, I definitely got a mouthful about. Imagine if she knew about the drunk driving incident.

Another weather alert blares from all of our phones.

TORNADO WARNING
SEEK SHELTER IN A SAFE BUILDING
Recreational vehicles, mobile homes, trailers are unsafe
TAKE COVER NOW

"Great. Just fucking great!" Maddie gasps, pointing toward the front entrance at the rain battered windows. "See, now there's an actual tornado out there!"

"Maddie, we'll be fine in here. Just keep moving," Eric says but I know he's not as calm as he sounds.

I am not calm either. I'm also feeling really stupid for dropping my keys in the dude's cell. I don't want to go back, but I need to. Those keys aren't so easily replaceable.

Eric opens the door to go back into the area where all the inmate cells, two medical rooms, and two security rooms are. The only bright side about going back to the dude's cell is that we are not just standing in all that cold bacterium filled water now.

"Be quiet," Eric whispers as he aims the dim flashlight at the floor and toward the stairs.

We go upstairs, passing the security room, then the medical room with the operating area until we reach an inmate cell at the end of the hall. We silently go in and slightly close the door. Maddie makes sure to tell us to keep it propped open so we don't lock ourselves inside.

As we stand in near pitch-black darkness (because Maddie also made sure to tell us to keep our phones off, even though we've had them off, so the guy won't see us in here), Eric peeks out through the little window on the door. We can see the light shining from the guy's inmate cell across the way.

"His door is still being held open by those books," Eric whispers. "We won't know if he's in there unless he left while we were downstairs."

"See, all we're doing is wasting time now," Maddie mutters. "And now we might get taken out by a tornado up here. We should go back downstairs!"

After a few minutes of restless waiting and Maddie muttering about our plan, Eric shushes her. "He's leaving the cell. Heading toward his left, our right. He's got his flashlight with him. He went around the corner somewhere. I didn't see the axe in his hand but all I could really see was the flashlight moving around."

"He probably walked over to wherever he's keeping Oliver and Danny hostage," Maddie's muttering again.

"Okay, I'll be quick while you two keep a look out." As much as I do not want to go by myself, Maddie should not stay here alone and I know Eric doesn't want that either. "Maybe the dude's axe will still be in there and I can take it while I'm there. Disarm the son of a bitch."

But before I go, Maddie must complain once more. "Great plan. Steal the axe murderer's weapon so when he comes back to his house, he'll definitely know we took it. That won't make him angry or anything."

16

L U C A S

MONDAY – 1:00 a.m.

Either the guy is a murderer like Maddie says he is or the dude is a creep who enjoys watching drunk people roam around the place... or Eric was right. He could have been defending himself from his home and that's why he held the axe up behind Oliver and Maddie the first night we were here.

Out of the three possibilities, I hope Eric is right. If he wanted to kill us, then you would think he would have done so the other night.

But I'm not naïve to the possibility that Maddie is mostly likely right. The dude could be responsible for Danny and Oliver's absence. I just can't believe Danny and Oliver are in danger. Maybe he found their phones after they left here. Whatever the reason, I just want to find them and get the hell out of this building already.

Just as badly as I want to find my keys... and the axe.

But I don't see either. My keys are not on the floor where I thought I dropped them. Maybe the guy saw them drop and picked them up after I left.

Are they on top of the nightstand where Maddie found the phones?

Maybe he picked my keys up and put them in the drawer. Not that I want to rummage around this nasty shit but I look anyway.

Nope. My keys aren't anywhere... but I did just find a pile of old photos of women wearing lingerie, tied up to some bed.

What a sick fuck.

Even as a man, I have no interest in looking at these. They aren't flattering. The women do not look like they were willingly posing in any of these.

These pictures must've been an inmate's sick collection that was left behind before the prison shut down.

Fucker probably jacks off to these.

I need to get the hell out of here.

Before leaving, I check around the bottom bed for my keys and the axe. I ain't touching those sheets on the bed that are tangled up. Brown and wet stains are all over. *Fucking nasty.* I use my foot to kick the sheets apart in hopes to find my keys.

Nope. No keys. No axe.

Last check— underneath the bed. Hopefully I kicked the keys on accident when I turned around last time while we were in here.

Bending at my knees, I lean down to look, careful not to let my jeans touch the dirty floor.

Blood stains...

I shine my cell phone light (because I left the dim flashlight with Maddie and Eric) to follow the stain... and oh shit, there's more blood...

Dark red blood trickles down the wall and onto the floor, creating a small slightly dried up puddle.

The blood doesn't look fresh because it's dark red and coagulated, like it's been there a while. Not long enough to dry completely though.

Neither my keys or the axe are under here. Only a couple pairs of large boots and sneakers with the words 'property of the prison.' Not Danny's or Oliver's shoes. Just the boots that I assume were assigned to the inmates— the same boots that I saw the dude wearing.

I pass my light around under the bed once more near the blood stain. A glimpse of yellow and blue catches my eye near the metal of the bed frame— *A beaded bracelet.*

The beaded bracelet that my son made for me in day care earlier today is laying on the floor...

But that's not the one my son gave me because mine is still on my wrist.

That means...

Amy was here.

Or she still is...

17

LUCAS

MONDAY – 1:15 a.m.

Back in the main lobby near the front entrance, the three of us stand in the cold flood again. This time, water has risen to just an inch below mine and Eric's knees, and an inch or so above Maddie's.

"You think Amy really gave her bracelet to Oliver?" Eric asks in a disbelieving tone because it *is* pretty hard to believe— that Amy would give Oliver something her own son made for her. Especially when Oliver isn't her kid's father. "Maybe this doesn't belong to Amy? Did all the kids in the day care make the same bracelet?"

"I—I'm not sure. I know they all made bracelets but I don't know if our sons just decided to make the same design."

I examine the yellow and blue beaded bracelet with the letter I, a heart and the letter U in my hand. She couldn't have given this to him because he was already missing before I saw her earlier.

"Actually, Amy couldn't have given this to Oliver because our kids made these today. If this is hers, then she must've come here to look for him after I talked to her... Or another parent was here which doesn't make any sense." I start pacing as I weigh my heavy thoughts. *Am I the reason Amy came here?*

She didn't seem that concerned about Oliver when I spoke to her today. She seemed more worried about the storm because of a hole in her roof and bad brakes in her car. Hell, given their relationship history, I wouldn't think she would so willingly want to come look for him on her own.

"I need to call her." I scroll over to her name on my phone. If we didn't share a day care for our sons, I wouldn't even know her number.

"It's ringing so far, not going straight to voicemail so her phone can't be dead. I guess that's a good sign. You hear anything?" I ask Eric and Maddie.

They both shake their heads. None of us hear the sound of a phone ringing around us. We don't even hear the sound of vibration anywhere.

Amy's voicemail comes up on the other end after a few rings.

"Let's keep moving," Maddie reminds us. She picks up her feet, splashing the water. "The longer we stand here, the more challenging it's going to be to move around in this flood."

"Wait, are you sure the other phone you found is Oliver's and not Amy's?" I ask as I call Amy again.

After five rings, her voicemail comes up again.

"I'm positive." Maddie pulls the phone out of her hoodie pocket and turns it around to show us the skulls on the back. "I know this is his because of the phone case. I commented on it the other day that he needs a new one. The skulls are wearing out. And Amy's phone would go right to voicemail instead of ringing when you call her if this phone was hers because this one is completely dead. Her phone can't be dead or turned off since it's ringing on your end, like you said," Maddie says.

"Keep calling her and we might find her phone somewhere in here," Erics says.

"Or the psycho will find it before we do, if he doesn't already have it," Maddie murmurs.

As we trek down the hallway toward the burned side of the building, the water rises just past mine and Eric's knees (and Maddie's thighs). Eric opens a door that I thought would lead to another cell until he shines the flashlight in a small workout room. The whole area is flooded out. A basketball floats in the flood. A weight rack is halfway underwater. No sign of Oliver, Danny or Amy. I don't hear her phone ringing in here as I call again either.

"Didn't y'all look around this side of the building when we first got here— when you made us split up?" I ask Maddie.

"No. We only got a few steps into the hallway before you got too scared to be alone and then Eric nearly got swept away in the flood outside right after," Maddie sighs.

"My poor baby!" Eric scoffs. "The impound lot better not be in the path of the flood. This night just keeps getting worse."

"We have bigger problems right now," Maddie sighs.

"Tell that to my insurance!"

"I didn't get scared. I found that door that led us—"

Suddenly the sound of the storm increases outside, stopping me from finishing my sentence. Thunder crashes, lightning cracks in the sky, the wind bangs against the building as we get closer to the charred stairwell at the end of the hallway.

I sent Amy a few texts, but she has not responded to any and they all remain unread.

"You're sure you didn't see her phone anywhere in the psycho's cell when you found the bracelet?" Maddie asks me, shivering. "This water is cold!"

"I was too focused on looking for my keys which I never found by the way. After I found the bracelet, I just got out of there quickly. I didn't think to look for her phone too."

"If her phone was in there, you probably would have seen it near Oliver and Danny's phones," Eric says to Maddie.

For once, Maddie doesn't have a comeback. She can't argue with that logic because Eric is right. Amy's phone would likely be with Danny and Oliver's too if the dude had it. I doubt he is carrying Amy's phone on him or else he would have turned it off already.

That's if Amy is even here.

Maybe that bracelet does belong to another parent...

If that's the case, then I'm all confused. Why would another parent be here?

The flashlight that we took from the security room is flickering on and off now and basically becoming useless. It's bound to die any minute, so we are left to use the flashlight on our phones again. At least we have three phones again.

No sign of our friends, Amy or her phone anywhere down here. Still no text back from Amy yet either. My messages are getting delivered but not read.

"There's nowhere else to go but up those stairs," Eric points to the charred stairwell. Way down the hallway, the steps are still intact, but the railing is gone completely.

"If that guy doesn't kill us with his axe, then I'm pretty sure those stairs are going to take us out instead," Maddie shivers.

I hate to admit it, but I think she is right. Either the stairs will come crumbling down the minute we step on them... or the tornado lingering around the area will be the death of us.

18

MADISON

"Guys, we won't be able to go much farther unless you plan on swimming," I shiver as the water splashes against my waist. Correction, I'll actually be the one swimming. We're halfway to the stairs and somehow, the water is rising.

"Just a few more feet until we reach the stairs, Maddie," Eric says.

As we are pushing through deeper water and darker territory, we briefly check inside each door that we pass by before getting to the stairs. I am not keen on climbing them because the only part of it that looks intact are the actual steps, but how safe can they really be to stand on? And how safe is the second floor above us over here?

"It's really hard to believe that Amy came here on her own to look for Oliver after I talked to her earlier today. I can't picture her doing that," Lucas says as we head toward the staircase at the end of the hall.

Some of the doors to the cells are closed and some aren't. Each of us point our phone's flashlights in the cells. Thankfully, Danny's phone is still on and does not have to be unlocked to use his flashlight or else we would be left with only mine and Lucas's phones.

No sign of our friends, Danny's truck keys, Amy or her cell phone anywhere.

Then again, the keys or cell phone could be buried underneath this murky nearly pitch-black water that we are dangerously wading through.

Alligators...

Fucking alligators...

As we get closer to the stairs, the possibility that an alligator can be swimming around in this floodwater heightens my anxiety even more. And it's a *real* possibility. Most of this floodwater is being pushed in here from the lake— the lake that holds dozens and dozens of gators.

My new fear will remain locked in my mind though. For my sanity and for the guys. No way will I bring up an alligator to them.

They'll either tell me there's nothing to do about it which is true, or that I'm right to be scared and so are they. And I prefer to not hear either response from them.

I'm just gonna push the thought of a gator swimming around my legs in the back of my mind.

Actually, going up these stairs to the second floor does sound like a great idea now as I think about it. It is better than standing in possible gator infested water.

Okay, maybe not *infested* but a gator or two swimming around near our feet and legs is possible.

Push the thought away, Maddie.

Just get to the stairs already.

"Amy seemed more worried about her roof and her car. I swear, she didn't sound like she cared about Oliver at all," Lucas sighs.

"I guess we don't truly know what their relationship is really like though. Maybe she didn't want to show you that she was worried about him and decided to come here to look for him before we did." I realize a tinge of jealousy must have fallen over my face or in my voice when I just spoke because they are both uncomfortably staring at me.

In an unnecessary effort to show his support, Eric puts a hand on my shoulder. I shrug it off.

"Wait... where was Amy's car?" Lucas thinks out loud. "There wasn't another car outside when we got here. She couldn't have pulled up after Eric's car got towed either because of the flood. I can't picture her walking in the rain to get here…"

"Speaking of, I still don't understand how my car got towed. I know I parked out on the main road, but I doubt a random tow company came by to take it away for fun. Cars only get towed if they're under a tow-away sign or if somebody calls on them. Someone had to call—"

"THE GUY!" I realize out loud. "He must've called to get it towed. He wanted to trap us here!"

"Yeah, well his plan fucking work—"

Suddenly mine, Lucas, and Danny's phones simultaneously blare with an emergency notification.

Just when I thought we were in the clear from the last tornado warning, I'm proven wrong.

TORNADO WARNING

Seek Shelter in an enclosed building or basement immediately

TAKE COVER NOW

Okay, the second floor doesn't sound so appealing to me anymore.

Either stand around with a possible alligator or two, or a few, swimming around our legs down here…

Or head upstairs to survive a tornado in an unsafe structure.

I hate everything about this night.

I never panic in this type of weather. But being inside this dark, hardly intact building with barely any battery left on our phones, in possible gator infested water, and that we're trapped in here with an axe wielding psycho is causing my anxiety to not only heighten. I want to jump out of my skin. Literally.

"Good thing we're in a covered building," says Eric.

"More like partially covered," I shriek. "And we are literally about to go upstairs."

"Okay, nothing we can do about a tornado right now. I'm sure we're fine. We have no other option but to stay here anyway. We are in the best shelter we can be in right now. We don't have to go upstairs yet." Eric tries to calm me down even though he knows his efforts are not working.

"You hear a phone ringing at all? This is the last time I'm calling her. I need to save my battery." Lucas helplessly tries calling Amy again before taking the phone away from his ear. "Voicemail."

"Wait! I just heard something. Call her one more time," I say.

He calls again. We stand as still and silently as possible to listen for a phone ringing or vibrating, but all we hear is the violent wind outside and the subtle whooshing of the water surrounding us.

Sighing, I say, "I really thought I heard something."

"I think you just want to hear her phone ring," Eric says and he is not wrong.

He's not right either. I don't want to hear Amy's phone because that means she really was or still is in this building, and if she is still here, then she is most likely in danger. I don't like the woman, but that does not mean I want her to get hurt. If we do find her phone though, I can only hope that we will be a step closer to finding her with Danny and Oliver too.

We've checked almost every room and cell in here— where the plywood is allowing all the floodwater to come into the building. There's only one more door to open that is right next to the staircase at the end of the hall. Probably another cell but then again, the door looks different from the others we've already passed.

Before we reach the stairs, I realize the water starts to recede a bit right in front of that last closed door. I wonder why the water is starting to recede all of a sudden until Lucas pushes open the door and water rushes in... but downward.

"Uh, this doesn't look like an inmate cell," he says just as the floodwater flows through the open doorway, over dark descending stairs that lead down into a basement.

1 9

M A D I S O N

MONDAY – 1:38 a.m.

After Lucas opens the door, he only makes it a few steps past the doorway before abruptly stopping. Eric and I stumble over our feet and slam into each other.

"What the hell?" Eric gasps when I shine my phone's flashlight ahead of us on an absolutely pitch-black descending staircase. The floodwater from the hallway behind us rushes through the doorway, underneath our feet and down the concrete steps.

Then a loud splash startles me followed by a hiss.

I turn around and point my phone's light at the water. A tail whips ahead of me.

Gator...

Gator...

Fucking Gator.

"Gator," I gasp loudly and push my brother into Lucas, so I can get the door closed behind me.

"I knew it. I knew that could happen," I mutter, breathing heavily.

"What?" Lucas looks at me, confused.

"Nothing." Shaking my head, I stand on my toes to peer out of the small window on the door. There it goes. A literal alligator is swimming away from the door, down the hallway.

"Wait a second..." I attempt to turn the knob on the door because I have a bad feeling that we just locked ourselves in.

And for the near tenth time of the night, my instincts are proven right again.

The door doesn't budge. Of course it locked on its own. Of fucking course.

"We're locked in."

"Great. Now we have no choice but to go down here," Eric sighs.

"Well, would you rather have stayed out there with the gator?" I retort.

"Are you sure you saw a gator?" Lucas asks.

"YES!" I shout. "I saw the tail!"

Eric shines Danny's flashlight on the steps. "Oh, shit..."

Blood.

Blood mixed with a bit of the floodwater trails down the steps and along the walls down into the descending darkness. From where we stand, there isn't even an end to the stairs in sight.

"Oh fuck," Lucas mutters.

"We're trapped. We're literally trapped!" I involuntarily let a few tears escape my eyes. I am normally not a crier but this night is testing how mentally strong I am.

"Maddie, relax. I'm sure we'll get out of here eventually." Eric tries to comfort me once again.

And again, his optimistic attitude does not work on me.

"Bro, I'm about to shed some tears too," Lucas says.

Looks like Eric's optimism isn't working on Lucas either.

"Well, while we're stuck here, we might as well go look down there first. Then I'll break this door down with the baton stick when we want to get back out, okay?"

"Do you not see the blood ahead of us?" I shriek, pointing the stick toward the stairs. "And this is a metal door! Pretty sure you can't break that down. And are you forgetting about the damn gator?"

"Just stop worrying right now. We'll get out of here. I promise." Eric begins to walk down the steps.

I follow him while gripping onto the back of his shirt with Lucas leading the way down the dark descending steps.

"Hey, at least we know we're really safe from a tornado now." Eric lets out a nervous laugh.

I hate to admit it, but he is right. A basement is known to be the perfect place to seek shelter from a tornado which is clearly what these steps are leading us into.

Although as I think about it, how safe can it be down here for us?

Basements aren't so common in Florida. Yes, they can exist in Florida but they are not normally built under this type of terrain. This is a basement in the Everglades... in swamp territory.

Swamp territory equals gators.

And how well can this basement hold up without it flooding out? And for how long?

Unless the basement is flooded out already... which again, means more gators.

Fuck.

We only make it about ten steps down the stairs with no end in sight. My phone is at twenty percent now, so I turn off my flashlight to preserve battery.

"What percent are your phones on?" I ask them.

"Danny's has nine percent left," Eric answers. "I should stop using the flashlight before it dies."

"Eighteen on mine," Lucas says.

We should've called for help a long time ago. We should have called right when I found Danny and Oliver's phones. Or better yet, right when we saw the psycho holding an axe in our picture.

"I'm calling 9-1-1," I decide. I know the police can't physically make it out in this storm, but at least somebody will know where we are and who we're locked in here with if I do get ahold of anybody.

I wish it were that simple though.

Although part of me knew calling 9-1-1 wouldn't be such an easy thing to do, I'm still aggravated when my phone shows no signal. The farther we go down the steps, the farther we'll be out of range.

Maybe if I take a few steps closer to the door, I'll get a signal.

Holding my phone in the air, I walk back up the steps. I check for signal at the top step which is only inches away from the door.

But no luck.

"Maddie, come on!" Eric calls out.

I turn back around to catch up to them down the stairs.

"These stairs must lead to underground tunnels that were probably used for transporting prisoners back in the day. There's got to be an escape route down here to get outside of the building," Eric suggests, which does not make me feel any more at ease as we continue down these never ending stairs.

How deep could this basement go?

"Even if we find a way out of the building from down here, the exit could be boarded up by plywood or blocked by the flood," I remind him, suppressing the urge to also remind him about alligators.

"But at least, we might find a way out and away from that guy," Eric says. "This is not the time to be negative, Maddie. I know you're a pessimist but sometimes, it would not hurt to think positively, especially right now."

Okay, Eric is slightly right. I sure as hell, will not tell him that though. Being pessimistic is not helping our situation right now. Although, I really can't help being myself. How can I try to be positive when this entire night has been nothing but the opposite of positivity?

The farther we head down the steps— the little bit of water that is receding, splashes underneath our feet, and the more that flight response in me wants to take over. Except flight is no longer an option. Flight hasn't been an option for hours now.

"Maddie, walk in front of me," says Eric, so I can walk in the middle of him and Lucas. Eric looks behind his shoulder toward the top of the steps that aren't even visible to us anymore, even with the phone's flashlight. "Just in case," he says.

In case the psycho really comes after us and murders us down here.

Either that guy is going to find us down here, a tornado takes us out, or we find a flooded basement full of alligators, we are screwed either way. There is no way I can think positively right now. I'll leave that job to Eric.

We almost reach the end of the stairs when Lucas trips and nearly falls head first down them, but he steadies himself by holding onto the wall as I grab onto the back of his shirt.

"Damn, I almost rolled my ankle on something," he says. He points his phone's flashlight toward the floor near his shoes and to all of our surprise, a cell phone sits face down on the step. He picks the phone up and turns it over to look at the screen. His eyes widen when he clicks on the side button and the screen lights up. "This is Amy's." He shows us the wallpaper on the screen— a young boy with hazel eyes smiling with a watermelon in his hand. "That's her son... This is her phone."

I look back over my shoulder, past Eric at the darkness above us, shuddering.

"Guys, we need to keep going. If we keep standing here, I'll start crying again," I tell them and I mean it.

I don't want to stand here like bait. The eerie sensation and the urge to choose flight that were once running through my veins are far out of my body and replaced with pure panic. We need to keep moving, no matter where we end up. Whether the guy is above us or below, we just simply can't keep standing here.

Lucas pockets the phone and continues leading us down about ten more steps until we reach the entrance of a tunnel. "Well, here's the tunnel you mentioned," he says.

About ten more feet of walking in pure darkness besides the phone's flashlight feels like an eternity. My grip tightens around Lucas's shirt until we spot a light illuminating the area ahead of us— It looks like the same light that shone out of the psycho's cell upstairs.

"Oh... shit..." Lucas stops walking once we get closer. "No..." His voice expresses a sense of fright— a tone I have never heard in his voice before.

Then I walk ahead of him, regardless of Eric trying to stop me when I see a woman.

In the gleam of the light ahead of us at the end of the tunnel, a woman is chained on top of a metal operating table.

2 0

E R I C

When I suggested that tunnels were down here to aid prisoners in escaping, I expected to see actual tunnels. Not just one tunnel that led us out to a large spacious dark basement... And I definitely did not expect to find a pile of dead women in a large prisoner cell that resembles a human sized birdcage.

I also did not want or expect to see Amy, stripped down to only her bra and underwear, chained to a metal operating table. A knife is left stabbed in the middle of her stomach, a pool of blood seeping around it, dripping down her body, and splashing onto the floor.

The metal operating table looks the same as the table we saw in the medical room upstairs.

"No, no, no, no..." Lucas rushes over to her. The tears he mentioned suppressing earlier are starting to show. He shines his phone over Amy's face. She's pale, eyes closed and unmoving. "Fuck, man!"

"Oh my God!" Maddie gasps before covering her nose with her hands.

The stench of the room is ripe— a stench worse than what smelled out of the guy's cell upstairs.

Several battery powered flashlights, (same as the dim flashlight we found and the one that the psycho had) are setup on the floor and on two small nightstands.

We wondered why we couldn't find more flashlights in the security room and now we know. They're all down here.

"Amy! Amy! Amy!" Lucas presses two fingers against her neck to feel her pulse before putting his ear against her chest.

"She's not breathing. She's... she's d— dead... There's no pulse..." He steps back, face pale as I've ever seen it. "Her poor s-son... I feel— I feel terrible. She only came here because I told her Oliver was missing. I'm the reason she's— she's dead."

He starts pacing back and forth, hands on the back of his head, sobbing and muttering about Amy's son having to learn his mother was murdered.

But Amy's death is not the fault of Lucas. It's *my* fault because I am the one who told him to talk to her about Oliver. If I didn't tell him to talk to her, Amy wouldn't have known to come here. She would not have known that Oliver was missing.

"I'm the one who told you to call her," I tell him. "It's not your fault. Don't blame yourself."

As I stare at Amy's lifeless body, I wonder why she isn't piled in the cage with the other women.

Then again, those women look like they've been dead for a long time— not long enough for their bodies to be decomposed completely though. But it is clear, they have been dead here long enough.

I think Maddie might be thinking the same thing as I am because she is staring open mouthed at the cell full of dead women. Or she's not thinking at all and she might be completely in shock. Lucas is definitely in shock. He keeps pacing and mumbling. I've never seen him so distraught.

I need to think for all of us. We can't just stand here like sitting ducks. There has to be a way to get outside from down here, even in the flood. I rather risk the weather outside than face a murderer.

"She died because of me," Lucas mutters. "I shouldn't have told her about Oliver. This is my fault."

I put my hand on his shoulder. "No, it's not. I'm the one who told you to talk to her. Don't blame yourself for this. This is... this is fucked up, but we got to keep moving and find a way out of here. We can't stay here. There is nothing we can do for her now."

I turn around to check on Maddie. She picks up the large flashlight off the floor. She points the light around the corner of the cell that is holding the dead bodies.

"Another tunnel!" she gasps.

More blood trails down another tunnel that none of us noticed until Maddie just pointed it out.

"If Amy's down here. Then that means—" Maddie warily looks at us before she suddenly shouts, "DANNY! OLIVER!"

I exchange the same confused wide-eyed glance that Lucas holds. Maddie was so worried about making noise this whole night and now she is screaming for our friends in a dark basement down a tunnel that she has no idea where it leads to.

"Guys, Amy's dead. Oliver and Danny have to be down here somewhere too! And they're either dead already or they were next on that psycho's list. Time to start thinking realistically. Start calling their names!"

21

L U C A S

MONDAY – 1:55 a.m.

How am I going to face little Taylor after today? How am I going to explain what happened to his mom to my own son? How the hell am I going to explain this night, especially Amy's death to anybody?

Maddie has been right about this entire night after all. But she can't be right about Danny and Oliver possibly being dead. Despite how we just found Amy, I refuse to believe that. Danny and Oliver can't be gone too. They're alive. *They have to be.*

It is not until I turned my attention away from Amy to follow Maddie and Eric down the next tunnel, when I realize I think

I've seen those other women before. They look like the women in the photos that I found in the drawer of the dude's cell. I thought the photos belonged to an inmate before the prison shut down, but I think I was wrong. I'm pretty sure I was looking at images of dead women without even realizing it. Or the pictures might have been taken of them before they died.

I wouldn't know because I'm not a sick fuck like that psycho. I had no desire to keep looking. I only glanced at the photos briefly before finding Amy's bracelet and I got the hell out of there.

Now that we have a large flashlight to provide us with enough light, we can keep all of the flashlights on our phones off to save battery. Good because mine has fallen to ten percent now and I cannot allow it to die. I hope to God that my ex-wife hasn't tried to call me.

I follow Eric and Maddie down the second tunnel— This one is just as dark and even more narrow, but shorter in length compared to the first tunnel. The farther we go, the more blood we see and even more sense of dread takes over my body. I just want to find Danny and Oliver and a way out of here.

About fifteen steps in, Eric leads the way out to the exit of the tunnel into another room that is the size of a bathroom. The trail of blood has diminished into just drops and puddles scattered all over the floor.

A flashlight that is turned off is placed on the floor next to a visitor chair, and a bunch of cardboard boxes are stacked up against the wall in this room. It looks like the only way to get out of here is to backtrack through the tunnel we just came in through.

Maddie bends down in front of a small puddle of blood near the boxes. "This— this isn't good," she gulps. "This is the end. There's nowhere else to go. Where... where do we go? What do we do now?"

"This can't be the end," Eric says while pointing the flashlight around the small room. "There had to be a way for the prisoners to escape down here. The tunnel wouldn't just end here. There must be a secret way out of this room that's unseen from here and on the outside of the building. The exit has to be hidden."

While Maddie moves her phone around in the air in a desperate attempt for signal, I grab the flashlight off the floor and turn it on.

If Eric is right— that these tunnels were made for prisoners to escape the building, then the exit is probably hidden, like he just said. We need to look for a trap door or something. I shine the flashlight at the wall, opposite of where Eric is shining his.

"The prisoners would've had to escape toward the side of the building where there isn't a fence or any part of the outside that is enclosed," I say. "The courtyard in the front of the building is fenced in and so is the back yard."

"But the side of the building where Danny parked his truck isn't fenced in," Eric says. He's thinking what I'm thinking.

"Danny! Oliver!" Maddie yells, her voice trembling with fear.

Eric sighs. "Maybe this would be the time we should stay quiet—"

Or maybe not.

A slight noise interrupts Eric. We all heard it... but the noise sounded muffled.

What was that?

Maddie looks at us, eyes wide. "You heard that right? Oliver! Danny!"

Again, we hear the same noise... but I can't pinpoint what the sound is.

I turn to shine my flashlight down the tunnel we just came in from.

"Danny!" I shout.

"Oliver!" Eric calls out.

"Guys!" Maddie yells.

Again, we hear the mumbling once more. The sound did not come from the tunnel that led us here...

"Why does that noise sound like it came from behind the walls?" Maddie presses her ear up against a wall.

"Because I think it did..." As Eric answers her, I come to the same realization. *There is a way out of this room.*

Eric and I both begin moving the cardboard boxes. We quickly realize they're all empty as we easily chuck them away from the walls.

And there it is— not a small trap door like I thought we would find, but a normal sized door with a handle. There is no padlock or any lock on it at all. Eric pulls the handle down. The door opens effortlessly.

But we quickly realize it doesn't lead to an escape route. Instead, we walk into another brutal scene.

2 2

ERIC

MONDAY – 2:20 a.m.

Danny. Oliver...

Wrapped in plastic sheeting all the way up to their necks, they both lay on two metal operating tables.

"Holy shit!" Maddie shudders.

"Maddie?" Danny gasps. His eyes are wide open, and although he should be able to move his head left and right, he remains still. "I knew I heard you guys!"

Unlike how we found Amy, there aren't any knives protruding out of either of their stomachs. No blood trickling off their bodies and on the floor. They aren't chained either. The plastic wrap keeps them attached to the table, preventing any movement.

"Oh, thank fucking God," Danny gasps. "I can't fucking move. I heard you guys calling me. I-I-I didn't think you guys would hear me... Where's Oliver?"

"He's right next to you," Lucas gulps.

"What? Where? Why can't I move my head? I thought I was alone down here. It's been hours since I woke up. Help me off this table, please!"

The sight of my friends wrapped in plastic just like mummies and Maddie's frighten state combined terrifies me until Lucas turns around to feel Oliver's neck for a pulse.

"Oliver's alive. He's just unconscious," Lucas says.

"I don't know how long we've been down here, but I woke up like this hours ago. Not sure how many hours though. But I've been down here a while... Is—is Oliver okay?" Danny groans. "My head is killing me. I didn't even know he was here with me. He hasn't said anything..."

I shine the flashlight over Danny when I see blood matted hair on the back of his head. The blood is almost dried up though, so that must mean he isn't bleeding out which seems to be a good sign... But how good of a sign can that be since he has been knocked out for so many hours?

Maddie runs over to Oliver. She looks up at me and Lucas with hopeful eyes. "Are—are you s—sure he's alive?"

The plastic sheeting crunches under my hands while I shake Oliver's shoulders, as I attempt to jolt him awake. "Man, wake up! It's us!" I shout.

Lucas begins unwrapping the plastic off Danny. Getting the plastic off him is not so easy as it looks though because of how tight the plastic is around Danny's body and attached to the table. Meanwhile, Maddie checks every single one of our phones for a signal in a desperate attempt to get us out of here.

But by the look on her face, it is apparent she has no luck.

As I shake Oliver awake, I don't see any noticeable wounds on him anywhere. No blood visible anywhere. No wounds on the back of his head. After several attempts of calling Oliver's name and even resulting to slapping his face three times, Oliver's eyes start to flutter open.

"It's okay. It's us." I try to reassure him when he shifts his eyesight from me, then down to his body, eyes widening in terror at the sight of the plastic. Unlike Danny, he can lift his head easily.

"Ah! Wh—what the fuck?" Oliver tries to lift his arms and legs, but the plastic sheeting prevents him from any movement at all.

He turns his head to the side to look at Danny. Even though he hears Oliver wake up, Danny isn't looking his way. He said he couldn't move, but his head is free out of the plastic sheeting. He should be able to still move it just like Oliver can... So why can't he turn his head?

I begin yanking the plastic sheeting off Oliver while Maddie helps Lucas rip the plastic off Danny.

Once Oliver is able to move his limbs, he sits up and helps me yank the rest of the plastic off his lower body. When he is able to move and sit up, Oliver swings his legs off the table to stand up.

"Ah, fuck!" Instantly, he falls to the ground, shouting in pain. "My leg... My fucking leg!" On the floor, he leans on his left side, groaning in agonizing pain. That's when we all notice the blood running down his right leg and a bone literally protruding out of his shin. The bone wasn't noticeable until he got free from the plastic because there were so many layers wrapped around him.

Lucas tears off the final piece of plastic around Danny's feet. Even though he is free to move now, Danny remains still, laying on his back.

"I—I can't feel anything..." Danny murmurs. "I—I can't lift my legs... and—and my arms! Am I moving my head?" His eyes move from left to right, frantically.

"N—no. You're not moving at all," Lucas stutters. "It's okay. We're going to get you out of here."

"*Paralyzed?*" I mouth to Lucas without Danny seeing me and he shrugs with a slight nod.

He mouths, *"I think?"*

Maddie directs her attention to Danny. "What's wrong? Why can't he—?"

I turn to glare at her, mouthing the word *don't* with my eyes wide. Her eyes fall down to Danny as she realizes what is going on. Then she turns around and begins to look around the room, shining the flashlight along the walls, near the door we just found to get in here. I think she's looking for a way out. But I'm more concerned about how the hell we are going to get Danny and Oliver out of here if do find the way out. And if there isn't an exit in this room somewhere hidden, then we might just have to face that guy with only the baton stick and a couple of heavy flashlights to use as our weapons.

Better than nothing, I guess.

Oliver groans in agony as he forces himself to get up from the floor to hobble on one leg. He grabs a piece of plastic sheeting and ties it tightly around his knee, creating a tourniquet to stop the bleeding.

Maddie comes up beside me and whispers, "I found a bunch of needles and little bottles of liquid medicines with the name succinylcholine on them in one of those boxes you moved from the wall. I don't know what that name means."

I thought all the boxes were empty but I guess I was wrong.

"Me either but it must've been used to paralyze Danny," I whisper, hoping he doesn't hear us.

"Hopefully not permanently."

Since Oliver is not paralyzed, then the psycho upstairs must have plans to come back here to do the same to Oliver. But then again, why wait so many hours if he does have a plan to paralyze him too? Why even paralyze Danny, take the time to wrap both of them on the tables, but not kill them?

Did the psycho wait to kill them because of us? Did our sudden unannounced presence stop him from finishing the job on Danny and Oliver?

That depends on how long ago they got captured. Maybe it was Amy who stopped him from killing them. It could have been a combination of all of us showing up here together.

We have no idea when and how Amy arrived here. There wasn't another car outside of the building besides Danny's truck when we showed up and we know she didn't come with Oliver and Danny.

Oliver. Shit... I don't think he has any idea that Amy's dead. He might not even know that she's here at all.

"What happened when you guys got here?" I ask them.

"You saw the dude with the axe, right? He did this to you, right?" Lucas paces back and forth.

"Who else would it have been!?" Maddie retorts.

Oliver's eyes widen as he nods. "He saw you guys? He knows you're here?"

"Oh, he definitely saw us," Maddie mutters.

"What do you remember before you got knocked out?" I ask them.

"That asshole came up behind us when we were looking around the second floor for Danny's ring," Oliver groans as he leans against the table. "We were only here for about an hour, maybe a little more, before I felt something heavy hit the back of my leg right after we went to look in one of the cells. I turned around to see the asshole hovering over me. He slammed the back of my knee with the blunt side of the axe.

"That's when I went down. The pain hit me hard, man. I tried to stand up when Danny turned around to tackle him. The dude slammed him in the head with the same side of the axe. I got up and tried to tackle him myself, but then he hit my head and must've knocked me out because that's all I remember. Shit, everything happened so fast."

"I didn't get knocked out when he hit me in the head though," Danny says. "I fell to the ground and then I felt something sharp stab me in my side. I think it was something to make me unconscious."

"Wait, did I get stabbed too?!" Oliver inspects his body in horror.

"What time is it right now? How long have we been trapped down here?" The realization that we are all here suddenly dawns on Danny. "We been here for a while, huh? That's why you guys came to look for us, I'm guessing?"

Maddie checks her phone for the time. "It's two-thirty—"

"In the afternoon?" Oliver gasps.

"No. At night. Well, morning. You guys have been here since Saturday night. It's Monday now."

"Fuck! Am I— Am I paralyzed?" Danny stammers. He shifts his eyes around frantically while he mutters in a panic. "Shit. I bet that's what he stabbed me with. Knocked me out and paralyzed me. What the fuck!"

"We need to get Danny to a hospital like right now," Maddie whispers to me.

Either we find a way to get outside from down here and brave the flood which will seem merely impossible with Danny and Oliver's injuries. Or we head back upstairs and face the deranged killer.

Out of the two options, I'd like to choose braving the flood but as optimistic as I am, I know that is not as practical as I want it to be.

"Danny, do you still have your keys on you?" Maddie asks, but I remind her the flood is too high. His truck will surely stall out, even if we get the engine running.

"What flood?" Both Danny and Oliver question in unison.

"We're literally in a tropical storm right now," Maddie sighs. "The roads are super flooded. Like badly. Eric almost died out there."

"I didn't almost die," I sigh.

"My truck isn't in the flood, is—"

"—Yes." Now it's mine, Lucas, and Maddie's turn to answer in unison.

"What a fucking night," Danny groans. "Get me off this table, please!"

"So even if we find an exit down here, we're not really out of here yet," Lucas says. "At least, not until the storm passes."

"Our best bet right now is to get back upstairs where we can get service on our phones and call an ambulance. I'll break through the window and unlock the door from the outside, like I said before," I say.

"Upstairs?" Oliver asks in disbelief. "Where the hell are we?"

"In a basement," says Maddie.

"What the fuck?" Danny groans.

"Maybe we'll find a key somewhere down here to unlock the door upstairs. I don't think you're going to be able to just break that thick glass open so easily," Maddie tells me and I don't want to tell her she might be right.

This is a prison after all. If it were easy to break the glass on any of the doors in this building, all the prisoners would have done it before… But none of the prisoners ever had a police baton stick like we do.

It has to work.

"How did you guys find us down here?" Oliver asks.

"By accident—" says Maddie.

"—By luck," says Lucas.

"They're both right." I briefly tell Danny and Oliver about how we ended up down here because Maddie saw an alligator and slammed the door shut.

"Oh, so it's Maddie's fault that we're locked down here then," Oliver nudges her and laughs despite the amount of pain he's clearly suppressing.

She punches his arm which sends him to hobble on his good leg. "This isn't funny. Did you want me to just leave the door open for the gator to accompany us down here?"

Before we decide to make the trek back through the tunnels and up those steps to the locked door, we do one last check in this room for another way out. The door that led us in here was blocked by boxes. There aren't any boxes against these walls. Nothing indicates there is a hidden door anywhere.

But still, each of us (besides Danny) run our hands and shine the flashlights along the walls when I realize we should check the ceiling. Basements normally have a ladder that should lead to an exit outside. I'm the only one out of our group that is tall enough for my fingertips to touch the ceiling.

But no luck. Our next option is to check the basement where Amy and the dead women are.

Shit... Oliver. He hasn't asked about Amy so I don't think he knows she's here.

"Uh, before we leave, I got to tell you something." I look at Oliver. "Amy's here."

"What? Why?"

"We think she came to look for you before we did."

"Where is she?"

"You're gonna see her, but she's... she's dead, man. I'm sorry."

"The fuck? Where is she?" His eyes widen.

I gesture for him to follow us as I pick Danny up from the table with Lucas's assistance. When Danny's feet touch the ground, he collapses onto our shoulders, so we share the responsibility of holding him upright.

When we are halfway into the tunnel to get back to the basement, Danny's bodyweight starts to feel a bit lighter around our shoulders.

"Holy shit, I can kind of feel my legs again," Danny gasps. "I'm starting to get the feeling in my legs back!"

"The paralytic must've been temporary," Maddie says as she holds Oliver up on one shoulder behind us. He hobbles alongside her.

"Pick up all the flashlights we can," I tell them with a plan to use each one as a weapon if needed. "That way we each have something to defend ourselves. Maddie, keep the stick."

"I didn't plan on letting it go," she murmurs.

When we make it out of the tunnel and reach the basement, I shine my light ahead on Amy. Oliver lets go of Maddie and limps over to her.

"It's my fault she came here. I told her you never came home. I shouldn't have talked to her," Lucas exhales.

"She's gone. I'm sorry," I say to Oliver.

He stares at her lifeless body in a state of shock. "Her poor son."

"I know. I've been thinking the same thing," Lucas says.

"Shh!" Maddie whispers even though whispering isn't needed because by the looks on all of our faces, I think we all heard the same noise— Heavy footsteps echo in the first tunnel behind us.

Maddie's eyes fill with tears. "He's down here."

23

MADISON

MONDAY – 2:35 a.m.

Something fast and small comes twirling right at us. A loud and sharp bursting sound fills the air at the same time. Out of instinct, we all duck down while shielding our heads. Each of us disperse, crawling in different directions.

As I take cover with Oliver behind the table that Amy's on, I spot Lucas pulling Danny down to the floor near the cell that is holding the dead bodies. Eric disappears somewhere out of my sight.

Another sharp and short bursting sound fills the air... but I know that wasn't the sound of a bullet. I have plenty of experience shooting guns at the range with Eric and my dad. We all know what a gunshot sounds like and that was most definitely not it. The sharp noise sounded similar... but still not quite it...

Again, a sharp sudden noise fills the room...

Clank.

Out of the corner of my eye, I catch a glimpse of a nail bouncing off the wall before it lands on the floor near me and Oliver.

"Nail gun!" I hastily whisper. "He's shooting nails at us!"

A nail gun isn't as deadly as a real gun but it can be equally dangerous if the nail hits the right spot on a person...

The sharp sound flies over our heads once again. I watch another nail bounce off the wall and land on the floor. This time, only a few inches away from us.

Every time he shoots, the nails just keep ricocheting off the wall and landing on the floor. He isn't standing close enough for the nails to actually penetrate the wall, or worse— his actual target, our heads. He's too far away.

"Ah! Fuck!" Eric shouts from somewhere across the room.

Or maybe the psycho isn't as far away as I thought…

I lift my head up from behind the table to see Eric gripping his right shoulder in agony. He is only a few feet away from where Danny and Lucas are. Blood covers Eric's hand.

But even though my brother is clearly injured, he abruptly gets up from the floor and runs straight toward the direction of where the nails are coming from— Right at the psycho standing near the entrance, axe in one hand, nail gun in the other.

When Lucas sees Eric move, he immediately gets up to run after him, leaving Danny on the floor.

Oliver is about to grab me by my hoodie to pull me back down to the floor with him when we see what's happening. But instead of hiding with me, he takes the baton stick from my hand, then gets up to run after Lucas and Eric.

All three of them are charging right at the psycho.

Another sharp burst flies over my head as I duck down to the ground.

Clank.

I crawl over to Danny as he attempts to stand up but falls back down almost instantly. Although the paralytic is starting to wear off his body, his movements are still incredibly slow. He's too weak to stand, so he leans on me as we struggle to shield each other from the incoming nails soaring over our heads.

But then a thud echoes the room and nearly shakes the ground.

Everything happens so fast; I can barely comprehend what happens next.

24

ERIC

The fucker is shooting a nail gun at us. A nail already landed in my shoulder and damnit, the pain is intense. The physical pain ain't no match to the adrenaline and anger running through me though.

This guy wasn't expecting me to get up and rush right at him after hitting me with the nail and that's exactly what I hoped for.

As I get close to tackle him, I catch a glimpse of the axe in his other hand. He swings it at my head. I duck out of the way when Lucas comes up from the side of him and tackles him around his waist. The axe falls out of the guy's grip and lands on the floor next to us.

In the midst of grabbing him around the legs and taking him down, I manage to kick the axe out of the way.

Together, we knock him down on the ground, but he keeps the nail gun firmly in his grip.

A loud sharp burst fills the air as he shoots directly into Lucas's shoulder.

I catch a glimpse of Oliver limping over from the opposite side of Lucas with the baton stick. He drops down on his uninjured leg and slams the fucker in the head with the stick, causing the nail gun to fall out of the guy's hand.

The guy gets a few punches in on Lucas's face while I keep a strong hold around the fucker's legs. This guy is a few inches taller and heavier than both me and Lucas, so it's a struggle to keep him down on the ground, especially with my injured shoulder. He attempts to kick wildly out of our grip until Oliver slams him in the head with the stick again. The baton stick bounces out of Oliver's hands.

"Fuck you!" Oliver shouts and follows up with several punches to the guy's face.

Lucas lets go of his waist and moves over to get the guy in a chokehold by wrapping his arms and legs around his neck. Blood spurts all over Oliver's hands as he keeps throwing punches to the guy's face. Blood splashes and falls down the guy's shoulders, all over Lucas's legs and arms as he keeps the guy in a strong chokehold.

When he finally stops struggling, his legs go limp but we can see he's still awake because his eyes are fluttering open and closed. Lucas and I both let go and stand up. We take turns stomping him over the head while Oliver crawls out of the way, breathing heavily and gripping his bad leg.

Lucas kicks the guy in the stomach. Then I kick him in the head three more times. Or maybe four or five, before Lucas and I back away, catching our breath.

But even though the guy hasn't moved, Oliver crawls over to grab the axe on the ground, then leans over the guy and slashes him in the face once more. Breathless, kneeling in a puddle of blood, he looks up at us. "We just killed a guy."

2 5

MADDIE

MONDAY – 2:45 a.m.

I just watched my brother and my friends kill a guy...

This wouldn't be the time to tell the guys *I told you so* but damn, was I right.

Well, I didn't suspect the guy to be a serial killer. I had suspicions of him being a killer, but I wasn't suspecting him to be an actual *serial killer*. I didn't think he was responsible for killing more than one person.

Shit, I don't know what I thought.

I just knew the guy was bad. I had a bad instinct about him from the moment we ran into him. And I knew we were putting ourselves in danger from the moment we returned back here tonight. Even before we ran into him.

I think I'm in shock after what I just witnessed... and am currently still looking at...

I watched my brother and my friends kill a man, but I still can't comprehend what I just saw.

My head is spinning.

I feel nauseous... but not nauseous enough to throw up. I can't even move from this floor right now.

Strangely, I feel relieved though. Despite mother nature trapping us down here... At least, we're safe from one threat.

If the guys hadn't killed him, either one of us, if not all, would have died tonight. And judging by the dead women in a cell down here, I suspect I would have been that psycho's first target.

I also assume that is the reason why Danny and Oliver are still alive. By the looks of how we found them on the table, compared to how we found Amy and the other women, I assume the guy wanted to choose a different

route when it came to murder. That
guy didn't look like he had any interest
in killing males.

"Holy shit," Danny murmurs and
it wasn't until he just spoke, that I
remember he is sitting next to me on
the floor.

"M--make sure he's d--dead," I
stutter as I manage to help myself and
Danny get up from the floor. "Make
sure he's not just unconscious. Check
his pulse. Make sure he's not
breathing."

All five of us are silent until Eric
leans down to check the killer's wrist.
He stands up, shaking his head. "I
didn't feel a pulse. He's not breathing
either."

"He shouldn't be alive after what
we just did to him," Oliver seethes. He
leans against the wall, groaning and
gripping his broken leg.

"Fuck, my shoulder!" Lucas
exhales.

"Yeah, mine too," Eric grunts.

With a deep breath, I bend down
to rest my hands onto my knees,
resisting the urge to throw up.

We just killed a serial killer.

Okay, I shouldn't include myself
because I did absolutely nothing to
help kill him. All I did was stare

helplessly at my brother and friends while they beat the guy to death but still, people are fucking dead down here! We're literally surrounded by a bunch of dead bodies!

Someone we personally knew, no matter how much we disliked her, is dead because of us. Then there's all these women... all these poor helpless women who probably didn't deserve to die either. And judging by the looks of their decomposed rotting bodies, I think they've been dead a long time.

"W—we killed him," Eric exhales, gripping his shoulder. Blood runs through his fingers, down his shirt and all over his pants. He steps back from the psycho's lifeless body, shaking his head.

"Fucking good!" Oliver scoffs. "He deserved to die."

"We need to get back upstairs to get cell reception." I pick up a flashlight that one of us dropped before we ducked for coverage from the nail gun.

"He must've saw us come down here," Lucas groans.

"Or he was coming back for me and Danny," Oliver says.

"I bet he used the nail gun because he wanted to take us out one by one," Eric says. "Five people against one person isn't the best of odds when that one person has only an axe, but a nail gun has a better chance of getting the job done."

"At least, he thought it would," I say. Then I finally let out what has been running through my mind while I search around the basement for the key to the door upstairs. "I was thinking he might be one of the inmates who escaped out of here during the fire. They never found a few of them, remember? I looked the inmates up but he didn't look like any of them that were pictured."

"Doesn't really matter who he was now," Eric sighs. "At least the threat is gone for us tonight. Now we just need to focus on getting the hell out of here."

Eric walks over to help Oliver stand up. He is limping even more now after straining himself in the fight.

"How you feeling?" Lucas asks Danny who is stretching his arms across his chest while moving his neck back and forth.

"I'm regaining more feeling," he answers.

"Wait... maybe the psycho has a key to the door on him." My suggestion causes all of the guys to stare at me like I've grown an extra head on my neck.

"Well, I'm not going to search him for it!" I cross my arms.

Eric kicks the guy's legs to make sure he isn't moving even though he just checked for a pulse minutes ago. And after the gruesome beating they gave him that I just witnessed, I can't imagine how anyone would survive a beating like that. When no reaction comes out of him, Eric quickly kneels down and inspects his body.

"There ain't any pockets in his uniform. If he's got a key, he's hiding it somewhere none of us want to touch," Eric cringes.

"Check his shoes!"

Eric pulls off the guy's right boot, then the left boot. Dirty feet, nearly colored black from grime and a smell as rotten as the dead bodies fills the airs.

"No key hiding in his shoes either." Eric turns his nose in disgust.

"He probably just left the door open upstairs," Lucas says. "Let's just get away from him. I'm gonna be sick if we stay here any longer."

So am I. Thinking logically, I'm hoping Lucas is right. The door has to be left open because the guy wouldn't purposely lock himself in here. Or he hid the key somewhere down here and we have no patience or time to look for it right now.

But then again, if he left the door open, we could face the alligator again.

Fuck.

Everyone besides myself, needs to get to a hospital as soon as possible. Oliver needs surgery for his broken leg and his head needs to be checked out after being knocked unconscious for so many hours. Eric and Lucas both literally have a nail stuck in their shoulders. Eric's hands and leg are still cut from the barb wire on the fence, while Danny and Oliver probably have a concussion. We have no idea what effects the temporary paralytic could do to Danny's body too. He's regained movement in his limbs but that doesn't mean there aren't long term effects on his body.

Down here, the storm isn't so loud but it must be getting worse because the radar earlier predicted that the storm would last until tomorrow afternoon. It's already way past midnight, so I know we're getting the brunt of the storm right now. Most tropical storms and hurricanes always have the worst effects at night. Even though, we probably won't get help right away, we still need to call the police and paramedics immediately. The sooner they know we are here, the sooner they'll come out to get us once it's safe outside.

"OH MY GOD!" I gasp, startling everyone.

"The fuck? What now?" Oliver groans.

"The ring!" I shout louder than I intended to when I pull Danny's ring out of the pocket of my jean shorts. "Danny! We found your dad's ring. Guess this night wasn't such a bust after all."

"Well, look who is being optimistic now," Eric scoffs sarcastically.

"Well, shit. I guess you are right," Danny huffs. "This whole night wasn't for nothing after all, I guess."

He takes the ring from me, puts it on his finger, and lets out a hysterical laugh.

2 6

<hr>

DANNY

All of this just to get my father's ring back. I am not sure if I should regret coming back here or if I should be relieved about the outcome of the night. Or if I should feel both feelings.

I have no idea how I should be feeling right now because if we never came back here for the ring, who knows how many more women that guy would have killed?

Then again, if we hadn't come back here at all, Amy would still be alive because the only reason she came here was to find Oliver after Lucas told her he was here with me. And I am the reason why Oliver was here in the first place. I could have come back here alone. Amy would have never come to look for Oliver then and she wouldn't have died.

I am sure my dad is looking down on me. He's probably both proud and disappointed in me at the same time. Disappointed that I was reckless enough to land myself in this mess. Proud that I refused to let go of the one thing that still connects me to him and proud that we stopped and killed an actual serial killer. Talk about feeling conflicted.

Hell, out of this whole night, I never even expected to get the ring back at all. I actually completely forgot about it when I woke up wrapped in a Dexter styled imitation of a victim until Maddie gave me the ring.

"Did you guys get into the building through the side door?" Maddie asks.

"Yeah. Oliver remembered getting in that way the other night, why?"

"Was it unlocked or did you guys break in?"

"It was unlocked when we got here. Why?"

"The psycho must've kept it like that then," Maddie says. "I was wondering why it was unlocked when we got here. I think he kept that door open for himself. I bet he dragged the women through that door we all went through and down here to the basement."

"What does it even matter now?" Eric groans.

"It doesn't. I was just thinking out loud," she shrugs.

"I can't believe you guys came back for us," Oliver says.

"Thank God they did," I say. Man, am I more than thankful for my friends caring enough about me and Oliver to come look for us. "We would have died if you guys didn't."

"Let's not speak too soon. We haven't made it out of this building yet," Maddie mutters.

With a flashlight in hand, Maddie leads us through a tunnel toward a set of stairs that lead up to the prison— I have no memory of this at all since me and Oliver were knocked unconscious when the guy brought us down here. I can finally walk, just not as fast as I want to, so I'm trailing behind, using the wall to aid in my ability to move. Lucas and Eric are helping Oliver limp on one leg in front of me.

We reach the staircase and after struggling to make it to the top step, we finally see the metal door they've been talking about. It's completely shut.

"Guess he didn't leave it open," Lucas mumbles as he steps in front of us to try to turn the knob.

The door doesn't budge.

"Watch out." Eric steps in front of us with the baton stick in his hand.

Right when he swings the stick against the window, the building suddenly shakes. A loud rumbling echoes around us. A series of lightning strikes rock the building. The entire floor under us feels like it's starting to move...

"Tornado!" Maddie gasps.

"Tornado?" Me and Oliver repeat in disbelief. "What tornado?"

Not only are we apparently flooded out and stuck here in a tropical storm, but now there's a tornado outside?

Oliver and I knew a tropical storm was in the forecast, but we didn't know how bad it would get and we of course, did not expect to be here when the storm hit.

"I did not survive an axe murderer serial killing psycho to get taken out by a damn tornado!" Maddie shouts.

But mother nature has no feelings. Our instincts take over. We all hit the ground and shield each other with our arms as the building violently shakes.

For what seems like an eternity, we hear trees snap outside of the building. Rushing floodwater whooshes against this basement door and spills through the broken window over us. A deafening clasp of lightning strikes. Glass can be heard shattering all around us. The noise is so loud, you could mistake the windows out at the end of the hall in the prison's lobby for being down here at the top of the basement with us.

Then suddenly, all goes quiet... Eerily quiet.

All of us besides Oliver, stand up. Eric shines the large flashlight out of the broken window on the door.

"Holy shit," he mumbles. "If I get this door open, we're going to be in a hell of a lot deeper shit than we are down here. I think we got to wait it out."

"Wait what out?!" Maddie cries. "We need to get the hell out of here! You can't open the door?"

"Well, I can open it, but—"

Maddie pushes him aside and stands on her toes to look out of the broken window with the flashlight. "Oh m—my God," she stammers.

My friend's expressions are intensifying my nerves. I need to see what it looks like out there. "Let me see—"

And oh, shit.

Yeah, no way are we going to make it out of this basement safely.

Half of the building is literally in the hallway... and I can see the gloomy sky! The flood has risen to reach halfway up against the doors on the inmate cells. Tree branches float in the flood and stick out of the side of the building... or more like inside of the building.

All I see is complete destruction. What was left of the mangled roof is gone. The plywood panels that once held up parts of the outside of the prison are now on the inside of the prison. It's a complete mess. A complete unsafe mess for us to navigate through. There's no way we can get out of here. We're trapped.

"Let me at least try to call the police and an ambulance. They need to know where we are." Maddie pushes me aside to stick her arm out of the window with the phone in her hands.

"Be careful of the glass, Maddie," Eric says.

"I know. I know." She struggles to stick her arm out of the window. "There's a signal! I'm calling 9-1-1. We should be out of here soon."

For once, Maddie seems the most optimistic out of all of us.

27

MADISON

MONDAY – 3:02 a.m.

An emergency alert blares on my phone right when I hang up with 9-1-1.

TORNADO WARNING
SEEK SHELTER IMMEDIATELY
TAKE COVER NOW

"Not again!" I groan. "Why can't this night just be over already?" I cry out. *I will never say tropical storms are no big deal ever again in my life.*

Almost instantly, the wind howls again. This time, the sound of mother nature is ten times louder since the building is already disturbed and heavily deconstructed.

I scream; my voice buried in all the noise of the loud wind as we all hit the ground again, instinctively using each other to shield ourselves in the best way we can.

The wind whips viciously above us. Trees snap all around. The whole building sounds as if it is collapsing on top of us. Although by the looks of what I just saw from the first tornado, it seems like the building is physically impossible to collapse any more than it already has. The staircase below us shakes violently.

I thought we survived the night... until now.

If we aren't going to die in this tornado, we might just get buried alive in this stairwell.

2 8

OLIVER

The next day

The aftermath of a tropical storm is unbelievable. Shades of blue, pink and yellow decorate the evening sky. The sun is now shining over the horizon as it's getting ready to set and the weather is back to its normal eighty-five-degree temperature outside. Even though I have lived in Florida my entire life, I still think it's absolutely crazy how our town was hit with over sixty mile per hour wind gusts only yesterday. Now the wind speed has decreased significantly.

As I look out of the window from my bed on the second floor in the hospital, I can see that the trees are barely even moving. It took a long five hours until air rescue came to pick me and my friends up from the prison yesterday. The hospital we all got transported to is only twenty minutes from home, but this area got hit by one of the two tornadoes that touched down in our hometown too. Other than what I can see from my bed, which is only the horizon, I have no idea what it really looks like outside— how many buildings are destroyed, and how many roads are flooded out. I don't even know what our town looks like after the storm.

If Maddie never got through to 9-1-1, we would have most likely still been stuck in the basement and I can't even think about what could have happened to us— how long it would have taken for someone to find us. Or how long it would have taken for us to escape because nobody actually knew we were down there.

Let alone, nobody even knew we were at the prison. Nobody would have ever checked inside of the building for anyone after the storm either because no one was supposed to be in the building at all.

Having a broken leg ain't for the damn weak. I've been out of surgery for my leg for hours now. Slowly, I am starting to feel better after coming off the morphine. This is my first time breaking a bone and wearing a cast and it better be my last. I am not okay with being laid up in a bed like this, basically temporarily crippled. I haven't tried the crutches that are against the wall in the corner of the room yet and I have no interest in touching them.

But as much as this sucks, I have no room to complain about anything right now, especially a broken leg. At least there aren't any long-term side effects or concussions from whatever that psycho stuck me and Danny with. Thankfully, he isn't permanently paralyzed too. At least we all made it out of the prison alive.

Well, not all of us.

Although the survivors guilt weighs heavy amongst all of my friends, I know that Amy only died because of my choices.

Lucas blames himself for Amy's death because he told her that I was missing. Eric blames himself because he told Lucas to talk to Amy about me. Meanwhile, Maddie believes Amy's death is her fault because apparently, she gave Eric the suggestion to tell Lucas to talk to Amy.

But Amy's death isn't the fault of any of my friends, no matter who suggested what or who talked to who.

Everything that happened to us was *because of me* and nobody can convince me otherwise. Everything that happened in the prison was because of my shitty choices. Had I never brought us to the prison to begin with the first night, we wouldn't have dealt with all that we did. Danny would never have lost his father's ring. He wouldn't have had to go back for it and we never would have come face to face with a serial killer. My friends wouldn't have had to risk their lives to save us in a storm. And none of us would have faced death so many times in one night.

I was never in love with Amy. We were far from expecting to spend the rest of our lives together, but I still cared about her. I cared enough to not wish death upon her, especially in such a gruesome way.

If I want to find a silver lining in the whole night, then I guess stopping a serial killer from murdering more women would be it. If we never showed up to the prison and found those dead bodies, more women would have been murdered. And basically, killing him not only saved our lives but avenged Amy's death too. Killing the guy is what I am proud of and I don't feel guilty about one bit. I only feel guilty as shit about Amy. Nothing is going to change that.

My nurse just left the room a few minutes ago. Thankfully, she likes to gossip when I asked how my friends were doing because my phone has been dead this whole time. She just got me a charger, so I'm waiting for my phone to charge enough to turn back on.

In the meantime, she filled me in about the guy we killed— *The Everglades Killer,* deemed by the local news. Apparently, he was an escaped convict from the prison.

I'm sure Maddie is dying to let us all know she was right about him. I faintly remember her babbling about wondering if he was an escaped inmate or not when we were trapped in the basement.

Which speaking of, here come my friends right now.

"Ah, you're awake!" Lucas says when he walks into the room with Eric. Both of their shoulders are bandaged up from getting shot with the nail gun. Maddie, who is unharmed physically but most likely mentally traumatized pushes Danny in a wheelchair behind them.

"Did the detective come in here yet?" Maddie asks. She sounds anxious.

"No, not yet. The nurse just told me that psycho's all over the news. My phones dead. It's charging. I haven't looked the story up yet. He's called the Everglades killer or some shit? Why would the detective want to talk to me?"

"Because Amy didn't come to the prison to find you," Maddie says.

"Then why was she there?" I shift uncomfortably to sit up a bit in the bed. *Bad idea.* Although my leg is the only limb physically broken, every part of my body aches too, especially my hands.

"The detective said the guy picked her up outside of the bar. She pulled her car over on the side of the road in the rain a few hours after Lucas talked to her," Maddie says, swiftly.

"Okay, wait. Rewind," Eric stops her. "Let me explain better. The detective told us that Amy was seen on the bar's security footage about an hour before we went to the prison to look for you and Danny. She pulled over outside of the bar."

"I think she pulled over because her brakes weren't working well in the rain," Lucas interjects. "She told me they didn't work well at the day care earlier that day before the storm came. Taylor wasn't with her so she must've been on her way back from dropping him off at his dad's."

"So, when she pulled over, the cameras outside of the bar caught the guy— the Everglade's killer, whatever the news wants to call him, coming out of the woods and up to her passenger window. It seemed like her door was unlocked because he just opened it and got right in. Then the car drove off right after," Eric says.

"We assume the dude talked her into driving him to the prison, and well, you can guess what happened after," Lucas says.

"So then... it was just a coincidence that she ended up being a victim in all this?" I can't wrap my head around this. *What the fuck? Talk about a small fucking town tragedy.*

"Seems like it," Maddie answers. "Apparently the police were investigating a bunch of disappearances outside of town. They didn't link it to the guy until last night when we told them about him."

I look at Danny. "So that means he took her back to the prison while we were already there. Why didn't we hear them then?"

"He brought her back there hours after you guys were knocked out," Maddie says. "Literally right before we got there. Oliver, you were knocked out. Danny was awake but he couldn't hear from where you guys were in the basement."

"Shit," I mumble.

"Sorry, man. We shouldn't have gone back—" Danny says, but I stop him from blaming himself.

"No, I'm sorry. We only went back because I brought us there the first time."

"Alright well, let's not start playing the blame game again," Eric interrupts. "At least we know Amy didn't die because of any of us. It's still sad that she died but—"

"—But I keep wondering why the dude didn't kill us though. Why did he knock us out and temporarily paralyze me, but not kill us right away?" Danny thinks out loud. "And he left us down there for so long. That makes no sense."

"I don't think he was prepared to kill you in the way he usually killed his victims," Maddie says. "He was used to killing females.

There were only dead women down in that basement. I don't think he was ready to kill a male, let alone two men. And I'm just assuming, maybe he wanted to torture you guys since he wrapped you in plastic and left you there. I mean, I don't think he had experience using the medicines he used on you. I think he was just having fun with what he found in the medical rooms. The guy was clearly a sicko."

"Yeah, no kidding," Lucas huffs.

"Since he knocked you guys out the night before and didn't leave the prison to go get Amy until the next day, then I think he either forgot about you guys after he took you down to the basement, which I think would be stupid on his part, but then again killers aren't as smart as they think they are," Maddie says, "Or he just didn't care about leaving you guys there alive while he moved onto killing Amy. Maybe he didn't know the paralytic he used on Danny would eventually wear off."

"Then when we showed up, the guy—"

"The killer, you mean," Maddie corrects Eric.

"The killer, whatever, he probably got all sorts of fucked up when he saw us. He probably didn't know what to do or who to kill first," Eric adds.

"Well, shit," I shudder. "I don't know how to feel. I'm kind of glad Amy didn't care that much about me to come look for me but she still ended up being there. How the fuck?"

I didn't love Amy but I didn't want her dead. Occasionally, we exchanged strong words, but never to the extent of wanting each other killed.

"Am I selfish for feeling sort of relieved that she didn't come on her own to look for me? I really don't know how I should feel right now," I say.

"Not at all," Lucas says. "We're all feeling some sort of relief. It's a weird situation. I just keep thinking about her son now. He's going to grow up without his mom around."

"Yeah, we're all thinking about that," Danny says. And I realize, out of all of us, Danny relates to Amy's kid the most. Danny is the one who grew up without a parent in our group and now he's going to live the rest of his adult life without the other.

To my dismay, I hear a clank on the floor which startles all of us until we realize Danny dropped his ring.

Maddie bends down to pick it up and hands it to him. She scoffs a laugh. "Never lose this damn thing ever again."

2 9

B R E A K I N G   N E W S

Just hours after the tropical storm that carried two tornados, an EF1 and an EF2, ripped apart our small town— a wanted prisoner escapee has been found and is confirmed dead in the Blackridge Penitentiary—a maximum security prison that caught fire and shut down seven years ago.

Carl Dreary was one of the six inmates who managed to escape when the fire broke out. He was never found until last night when a group of individuals ventured into the prison to seek shelter from the storm.

What they encountered ended up being an entire night of survival, not just from the storm which brought on two damaging tornadoes, but from Dreary too.

Along with Dreary's deceased body, ten other women have been found deceased in the Blackridge Penitentiary, naming Dreary the *Everglade's serial killer*. Seargent Brookes of Everglades City has confirmed that the everglades serial killer hunted for his victims in our very own city, and the surrounding towns.

Along with the bodies found in the basement of the penitentiary, several vehicles were found discarded a couple hundred feet behind the prison, hidden away in the mangrove forest.

So far, the identities of each victim have not been confirmed yet besides one.

In a strange turn of events, the five individuals who have yet to be identified publicly, found Dreary's most recent victim's remains, *Amy Marty*—age thirty-one years old, while they were seeking shelter in the penitentiary from the storm. They also went face to face with Carl Dreary who is now confirmed to be deceased.

This is a developing story.

3 0

N O W

D A N N Y

Just when I thought I couldn't get enough death in my life, here I am at the bar, after leaving another funeral within only two months from attending the last one. Ironically, my friends and I are back sitting in the bar of where it all began. But my friends and I are not here to get drunk today. Only a few drinks this time. Just enough to take the edge off after all we've gone through, especially after just burying Amy only moments ago.

Ironically, this bar was not in the path of destruction because both tornadoes went the opposite way after ripping through the prison. A few trees fell down in the parking lot from the strong winds and missed landing on the roof of the bar. Now, the bar as it was always a hot spot in the town, is even more popular because it's the only bar (out of the only two in this town) that held up and is still in business.

Overall, the destruction from the storm in town is minor. Along with the prison getting wiped out, the other bar, two stilt houses, and a corner store got torn apart. Unfortunately, one person died in the corner store and two people were injured as a result from the natural disaster. It's crazy what a difference in a two-mile radius from where the tornado destroyed the prison did.

Then again, half of the prison was already burned down and the whole building was barely safe to stand in anyway, so it didn't take much for the building to completely fall apart. Ironically enough the basement nearly killed us and also saved us from the storm.

"You guys brought me here to forget about my dad's death before and look at where it got us," I scoff a laugh, which prompts my friends to follow just as our beers get delivered to the table.

"Dark humor at its finest," Maddie laughs.

My phone buzzes on the table from an unrecognizable number. Anyone who normally calls me is saved as a contact in my phone, so I have no idea who this could be right now.

"Hello?" I answer in a slight shout because the noise of everyone in this bar is growing louder. A group of people who were at Amy's funeral are starting to roll in.

"Mr. Leeway, this is Detective Coleman here. Do you have a minute to speak with me?"

"The detective," I mouth to my friends, scrunching my forehead. What could he be calling about now? I thought we were done with questioning regarding that Dreary dude.

"Uh, sure," I say as I put my phone on speaker and set it on the table.

"I'm calling regarding your father's hit and run."

"Oh," I reply without hiding the shock in my tone.

My friends all hold the same look of confusion.

"We have an update on who the other driver was," Detective Coleman says.

"I thought you already knew who the person was. You told me the other driver died in the accident too. His name was Rodrigo, right?"

I swear Detective Coleman told me that the other driver (the one who was drunk) died on impact during the crash that involved my father.

"We unfortunately relayed the wrong information to you and I deeply apologize about the miscommunication. The driver who we originally found in the other vehicle involving your father's accident was not responsible for your father's death. Rodrigo did pass away but due to another drunken driving wreck. When a witness called and reported the car accident, we had another report of a car accident involving a drunk driver around the same time in town. That report was a hit and run which was supposed to be your father's accident report. The reports got mixed up. The driver who was responsible for your father's accident wasn't at the scene when paramedics and police got there. Rodrigo was not involved. He was involved in another accident."

"Uh... huh?" I look at my friends who are all holding the same confused expression. I'm only on my first beer. There is absolutely no way I'm too drunk to comprehend what Detective Coleman is saying. "So then, what are you telling me? Rodrigo didn't kill my dad? Who did?"

This whole time, I thought the person responsible for the wreck was dead. Does this mean, the real person has been going around town unharmed? At times, they could have been near me, in the same store or at the bar and I hadn't even known? Is the person in the bar with me now?

"Rodrigo was responsible for another car wreck at the same time your father's accident happened. It turns out the driver who was responsible for your father's accident was a woman by the name of Amy Marty. A witness recognized her face after seeing her photo on the news. The witness didn't report it until now because she wasn't sure who the woman was or what her name was."

To say my friends and I thought we couldn't hear any more shocking information was an understatement.

"Uhm, uh, okay. Thank you." I end the call because there is not much more to say.

"What a small fucking town," Oliver huffs and chugs his beer. He waves over the waitress. "A round of tequila shots."

So much for coming here to not get drunk again.

About the Author

Sara Kate with a K, writes psychological thriller and crime fiction mystery books in her RV out of South Florida. Aside from writing, she enjoys rollerblading, photography, painting, and anything thriller/mystery related.

INSTAGRAM.COM/SARAKATEAUTHOR
FACEBOOK.COM/SARAKATEAUTHOR
GOODREADS.COM/SARAKATEAUTHOR
BOOKBUB.COM/SARAKATEAUTHOR

Acknowledgments

Thank you to my husband and my father for always being my first readers and honestly giving me their input on my stories.

Thank you to my readers and fellow authors who endlessly support me, especially everyone in the thriller author group on Instagram.

From the UK to the US, I'm forever grateful for each one of you, whether you are a reader, author or both.

As always, thank you to my reliable and recurring ARC team for reading and promoting this book honestly.

BOOKS BY THE AUTHOR

THE WOMAN I BEFRIENDED (Book 1 to THE WOMAN I WANT DEAD) – Several missing men. A suspicious neighbor. A pattern only Ellie sees.

THE WOMAN I WANT DEAD (Book 2 to THE WOMAN I BEFRIENDED) – A cat and mouse serial killer thriller.

HE THOUGHT I WAS HIS – A stalker thriller.

EVERYTHING LED ME TO YOU – A new adult romantic crime mystery/thriller.

ZOEY'S MEMORY – a medical mental health mystery.

THE UNSEEN AND UNINVITED – A thriller short story on kindle.

**TWISTED VOWS: A DEADLY
MARRIAGE OF LIES AND REVENGE**

You can find Sara Kate's books on Amazon, Barnes & Noble, Walmart, Target, Books-a-million, and other store retailers! You can also request any of her books to be stocked in your local independent bookstores.

If you enjoyed this book, I'd love to hear your thoughts in a review on Barnes & Noble and Amazon